FISH AND GRITS

BY

TINA SMITH-BROWN

For My Sisters

Roseanne Skipper

Glendale Reed

Patrice Smith-Sanders

Una Smith-Edwards

Catherine Smith-Hull

Who Are My Heroes Everyday

ACKNOWLEDGMENTS

When I started on this project I naively thought I would write a book, independently publish it, tell the whole entire world about it, then sit back and watch it sell, sell, sell. Wrong. Birthing Fish and Grits has been just as hard as I imagine birthing a human child would be, and like most new parents I hope it is not my last work of art. No delivery goes smoothly alone, and this one certainly did not.

I acknowledge that Jesus Christ is my savior, my friend, my supporter, and my internal guidance system. I can do nothing without the love and confidence he gives me.

Several people have given me immeasurable help throughout this process:

My Family - Jerome Brown, Jerome Washington, Christian Smith, Bernard Edwards, and Tyler Williams (who sat patiently many hours while her Tee Tee worked), who were my side-line cheerleaders.

My Readers – Diane V. Ross (researcher extraordinaire) Victoria Miranda, Pat Adams, and Marilyn Flynn for reading my work and offering honest, constructive feedback.

My Friends - Lisa Jane Erwin, Alexandria Erwin, Stephanie Houston, Sarah Hall, Charlotte Curry-Biggs, and Alex Jamison who always have my back (literally).

My Chef - Valerie Erwin of Geechee Girl Rice Café, who serves up the best fish and grits in Philly.

My Copy-Editor - Akiba Solomon who fights fair and honest.

Special Thanks to Lorene Cary who guided me through this entire process, answering my many questions, lifting my head when it dropped from exhaustion and fear, and with whom I can share this writer's experience.

FISH AND GRITS

Prologue

Sleep eludes me on this, our last night together. I give up after several hours knowing that it will be impossible. At exactly 10 minutes after every hour, dual spotlight flashes of red and yellow streak across my bedroom ceiling, lasting only for the few seconds that it takes the #23 trolley to glide pass. There will be no waiting passengers at this hour to slow down its momentum.

In the pitch black of my bedroom my heavy eyes fall on the white numbers of my alarm clock—3:00 A.M. Kala will be gone in the morning. I'd said goodbye as bravely as a 14-year-old girl who is losing her best friend can, recognizing the drastic change that will occur in our lives without her presence. I am the same age that she was when our father died but she was, and still is, so much braver. And yes, I am afraid for her, and for us.

The last four years have felt like a lifetime. A lifetime filled with tears and laughter and love always, even in the darkest of moments. She has taught me so much, insisted that I be educated, write poetry and short stories until my fingers hurt. *"Just 'cause you live in a jungle don't mean you gotta be ignorant,"* she preached to us on a daily basis. Because of her determination to see me intelligent, I won my school's spelling bee – was the only seventh grader ever to do so – and competed in the citywide contest coming in 5th place. This fall I will go to one of the best high schools in Philadelphia. She thinks I will be promoted to the next level by mid-year. But my pride is not in myself, but instead in what she has accomplished in me. It is a pride so intense that my head throbs. I think of her, trying to force a smile to my lips, as I struggle with the burning in my eyes, and the moan that threatens to burst from my dry throat.

Through my open window, the sounds of breaking glass, pounding fists, and drunken threats, mixed with female crying float in on a spring breeze. The concrete jungle shrouds me, wrapping me in her cold, brittle arms. And finally, I give my silent tears permission to fall onto my cool cotton sheets. At last I settle my reason for the lack of sleep. There should be more. A permanent memory of what we shared, how she saved us. So I write it all, to remember her.

One Fish

CHAPTER ONE – Hunger

I expected the nightmare to follow me into the new day. I mean you just don't see your father die on the kitchen floor and get up feeling the same about the world. But I did—feel the same that is. Last night's dinner had been mopped up, melting flesh and blood too, along with his grit-riddled, lukewarm body. My father's final act was to leave us with empty stomachs, but I'd witnessed no shame in the death veil that clouded his eyes. It mirrored his treatment of us when life still ran cold through his veins.

Memories warred against hunger in the pit of my stomach. The shards of his shattered Jack Daniel's bottle were gone, although the smell of the brown liquor still hung in the mid-August air. Felt strange, the sparkling clean floor and the household calm. It was too soon, too forgiving, and it took me a few moments to adjust to the saneness, which wasn't at all like our home.

My father's death, still brand new, had been a brutal event and I guess I should have missed him. But the growl growing louder by the minute in the pit of my stomach blocked out any serious thoughts of guilt. Besides, as I dragged a chair over to the dual windows facing the backyard, I wondered if things would get any worse. My sister, brothers and I had been hungry the day before and hungry again that day, only now I could hear our hunger a lot louder without the roar of his drunken voice in the background.

Elbows crusting heavy against the baking hot, crumbling brick at the bottom of the windowsill, I squinted as row after row of shirts, boxer shorts and blue jeans swayed in the stifling breeze. "One thing about living around poor folks, you don't know you're poor yourself," my sister, Kala, told me once, as we pinned worn-out clothes to our makeshift clothesline that we constantly had to make sure was secure.

Warm, sticky sweat trickled down the center of my back. We were in the middle of a three-week heat wave that caused thick vapors to rise up from the cracking sidewalks. A gray stray cat strolled past, his pinkish-white tongue lolling from a dry mouth. We glanced at each other with understanding. In the gigantic parking lot behind our row of homes, Mr. Jimmy, a self-made mechanic—a grease monkey as my father called him—slid beneath the belly of a scarred Oldsmobile. Kala said my mother had been with him—like most of the men in our neighborhood. I thought one day my father would kill my mother for it, but he never did seem to mind. His friendships were sealed with the cold beer and greasy rib sandwiches these same men purchased for him.

I once asked Kala why my mother did those types of things. She pointed to the inside of her elbow and shook her head like I should have been smart enough to know my own answer. That was one of the rare times I didn't like Kala very much.

The sweet scent of biscuits baking next door interrupted my train of thought and made my eyes water. Even in the midst of a heat wave, Miss Mickins baked biscuits every morning. God, I loved Miss Mickins. I fantasized about sitting at the kitchen table with her six kids, eating one of those fluffy light brown biscuits, butter and Karo syrup dripping off the crispy edges and onto my lips. But I couldn't hold on to the daydream; I was too distracted by the junkyard dog barking in my stomach, and the sight of my mother's hips as she switched toward Building Number One.

Two hours before, I had watched my mother tear up the bedroom she'd shared with my father, tossing dresser drawers and ripping closets apart. She glared at me, and then left the house to sell the one suit that my father owned.

An hour later, she returned with his pants tucked in a loose ball under her arm, disappointment spread like tar across her tawny skin. She looked at me accusingly then slapped me clean across the mouth.

"Nobody don't even want his old shit!" My right cheek burning, I'd turned away before she could see the loathing in my eyes and hit me again.

"Did get $10.00 for the jacket tho.' That was good, wasn't it?"

It wasn't the kind of question that required an answer, so I didn't offer one. She was gone again, before I had a chance to ask about what we kids were going to eat for breakfast.

Dizzy from heat and emptiness, my head dropped onto the paint-peeling windowsill. I sucked in a belly full of hot air. It didn't help. Only when I heard a screen door slam shut did I raise my head. Through

cracked eyes I watched as Noodle, the oldest of the
Mickins kids, dropped a bag of trash into their steel
garbage can and sealed it to keep out the rats, stray
dogs and such. He looked around quickly, taking in
the back of the concrete jungle in a few blinks. I
turned before his eyes could meet mine, ashamed of
the hunger swimming in them. Yet I hoped, crossing
my fingers until they ached, that he would notice and
offer me one of those biscuits. He didn't.

When the Mickins' screen door slammed shut for a
second time, I seriously considered sneaking out,
grabbing their trash, dragging it into our house and
eating whatever scraps I could dig up. But Kala
would've killed me – that, I knew. So I took another
deep breath and turned back to looking at ghetto
grass drooping over in the blazing heat. No chance
that it would survive on the mostly brown square
patches surrounding Fairhill Projects, our home. The
grass seemed to understand, as we did, that Fairhill
was a prison of sorts, the kind of place where you
don't recognize that you're locked in until you try to
venture beyond the five or six blocks that encompass
it.

My mother also understood the rules, but she
broke them regularly, stalking the concrete jungle
inhabitants like prey. Most folks slammed their front
door or closed their windows on her approach.

Looking out the window after her slap, I could no
longer see her swinging hips, her brown legs jutting
out of her bright orange shorts like leafless tree limbs.
She'd made it to the darkness of Building One's
emergency exit staircase, one of the places where she
chased her dreams. "She won't go far," Kala would
say at times like this. "Not far enough." But I never

worried about her disappearing for good because none of us ever dreamed of leaving; the concrete jungle was all we knew. My sister Kala was the only one who ever dreamed. She dreamed stuff all the time.

Kala had one of her dreams the night before my father died. We shared a bed and I was the only person she told about it. She'd whispered the dream in my ear, her morning breath just a little bit hot and funky.

"This time it wasn't 'bout life, but death," she said, her eyes huge and as round as saucers. *"I was flying over a forest of the saddest looking trees you ever wanted to see. Thousands of them, all squeezed together so that they couldn't breathe. They were topped with green, brown and red leaves that touched each other even when the wind wasn't blowing. Gigantic brown roots, exploded from the dirt beneath each tree creating a woody walkway that wound the trees together. Some of the trees were skinny and withered. Some small and new, but were bent downward toward the ground.*

Right in the middle of this forest, a group of seven trees stood separated from the rest, one much taller than the other six. I flew over that patch of trees and suddenly one of the smaller ones burst into flames. I watched in amazement as the flames from that little tree caught hold of the roots of the biggest one causing it to burst into a cloud of black smoke. Not fire, mind you, just smoke. The little tree didn't burn up; neither did the rest of the forest. But after that

17

big tree burned away to nothing but ashes, the strangest thing happened: The little tree stopped burning and raised its crown towards me in the sky. It wasn't looking down no more. Then suddenly this blue/green river appeared out of nowhere, and one gigantic, red fish just jumped right out of that water toward me in the sky. I woke-up crying 'cause I knew that dream was somehow about death."

That dream of Kala put fear in my heart 'cause I knew they always came true. I couldn't stop thinking of it, even that next day after death had visited our house.

I'd been at the window for about an hour and a thick mid-morning haze had settled in the sky. Kala approached in her bare feet, which smacked on the cracked linoleum kitchen floor.

"She gone again?" she asked, disgust sticking thick to the roof of her mouth like bad breath. I nodded my yes, my back still turned. Her small fingers brushed lightly against the back of my neck and I stood to face the question in her eyes.

"Yeah, she went to Building One," I announced.

"Well, I need you to watch these kids while I go up on the Avenue," my sister said in a no-nonsense tone of voice.
"Wha—what?" I stammered.

"I'm going for food," Kala said in a determined voice.

"Food?" I asked weakly, my knees almost buckling under the weight of the word.

18

She nodded, burying her hands so deep into her pockets that I expected she would pull out a chicken leg. Our eyes locked, her light brown to my dark, with complete understanding

In that moment, I thought of how everybody thought Kala and I looked alike. I suspected folks just didn't have anything else to say to members of a big family. With my dark chocolate skin and short afro, which I knew was on its way out of style, I didn't think I could hold a candle to Kala. Four years my senior, she has caramel candy brown skin, unsmiling light brown eyes and pretty long black hair supposedly inherited from our long-lost Indian relatives. At 14, Kala's face and body hinted at the incredibly beautiful woman she would become.

The three boys came after me. The twins, Sonny and Brother, who look and act totally different, followed by Baby.

Sonny, dark like me, is tall, lanky, and tripping over his feet all the time. Brother is a cross between me and Kala in coloring, short and stout, and full of false confidence. Sonny is eight minutes younger than Brother, who is two years younger than me, and six years younger than Kala.

Sonny and Brother are as opposite as turnip greens and collard greens, meaning they're in the same family, but with a totally different flavor. Where Brother is full of trouble and always seeking adventure, Sonny is quiet and prefers his own company to most. Sonny loves books like Kala, and he likes figuring out math problems that leave me with headaches. Meanwhile Brother has to get his knuckles cracked almost every night just to start his homework.

Baby, I think is the handsomest, with black curly hair and pudgy cheeks that would turn up into a wide grin whenever you said a word to him. He's not like any of us, being unique in his level temperament and good nature.

I'd cried the day the twins were born. Kala responded by slapping the spit right out of my mouth. But then she dried my tears and gave me a penny for a Squirrel Nut. I came to understand that the slap was her way of saying that we kids only had each other and had to stick together.

Days later, still rubbing my cheek, I wished that she could have just told me that, but then I might not have remembered it as well as I do today. I had foolishly worried that the arrival of the boys could make my father treat me worse, but by the time Baby arrived I understood that the boys' presence would not change anything. Separately, or as a group, our father treated us all with a cold distain.

CHAPTER TWO – Fish Market

Since I didn't take the trip with her, this is what I remember Kala told me when she got back. By the time she set out for the food, rumors about my father's death were already bouncing around the neighborhood. She said, "Like the Holy Ghost in a church full of sanctified folks: sweet to the lips and with just as much power."

It didn't take a rocket scientist, which I wasn't by any means, to know that folks would chew the gristle on this one for at least the next week—maybe longer if nobody else got themselves killed. Kala she'd just ignored the whispering lips, the shaking heads, the truths and the lies.

"I just pretended that their words didn't cut into my heart."

"Will it ever stop?" I asked her.

"Don't know. It's gonna be pretty hard to top dancing yourself to death," Kala reasoned. But I was sure that somebody in the concrete jungle was going to try.

As she left, our screen door with the missing screen slammed shut drawing the attention of a group of neighborhood girls, which included Sassy Mickins, my rival, from next door. They'd glanced in her direction, but wary of the cold look in her eyes and her "fighting reputation," quickly picked up their steps. On the porch, her lower lip trembled like it does when she's angry. That lip trembled a lot 'cause Kala was always angry. Not at us, only at the folks who needed somebody's anger, which she said was just about everybody else in the world. But that time I didn't think it was anger I felt vibrating from her soul. That time I felt for sure that it was fear.

It only took her about five minutes to turn the bend that led to the Avenue, which was teeming with Black and Asian folks—one group buying, the other selling. It was a game: the Black folks complained about the price and quality of the goods; the Asians offered to take 50 cents or a dollar off of the heavily marked up items.

With her shoulders straight, feet more marching than strolling, she'd swung more sass around that morning than Preacher Peifoy's daughter Ruena on Easter Sunday. She'd breezed past the Kresge's window displaying a pre-Halloween sale on holey, white *Friday the 13th*-themed hockey masks and wilting posters of President Carter shaking hands with the Shah of Iran. The yellow flag hanging between the items had a sale price of $5.

According to my history teacher, who had a brother being held hostage in this place called Iran, yellow flags were flying by the millions all over the country. She would cry a little whenever she'd talk about this, but the flag phenomenon never quite made it big in our neighborhood.

Her legs had slowed as she passed by the record store, which was blasting Michael Jackson's "Don't Stop 'Til You Get Enough." In front of Bee's Delicatessen, she'd tripped over a crack then giggled, "Almost broke my mother's back." A long line snaked outside of Bee's even though Rachel Brown claimed that she'd found a roach in the middle of her "American" hoagie last week.

At the end of the long block, the neighborhood's only supermarket and drugstore took up two corners, and the Rainbow Shop clothing store (which had a big grand opening two months before) and Nichols Shoes (the only shoe store that sent shoes to prisons) took up the others. The fish market, two stores before that corner, was a ratty old building, leaning more than standing. It was painted an ugly mustard color that resembled throw-up, and according to Kala "smelled like a thousand women on their period at the same time."

The large lettering on the market's sign read **KULMAN'S F _ SH**; the "**I**" had faded away long ago. Mr. Kulman was dead and his wife gone for at least five years, but the Koreans kept the name when they bought the place. "They just too cheap to buy a new sign," declared Miss Mathis (not the mother of Johnny Mathis, who I adored) from three doors down on the left. Everybody I knew agreed.

Kala said that when she got to the store, an ancient Korean man with weary eyes greeted her at the door. With a wrinkled hand he waved her inside and a bell tinkled overhead as she pushed open the door. "I hung back for a minute to just absorb the place," she'd boasted proudly. Walking between the two rows of wooden shelves loaded with vegetables, she landed at the steel and glass counter in the center of the store. From the corner of her eye, she'd spotted Billy Kettle, a one-legged vet wearing a faded olive army uniform, leaning against a stack of plastic crates smoking a Winston. He nodded, stared at her through half-cracked eyes, and smiled. She'd ignored his gesture.

Two women one tall and light with wild brown hair, the other short with Indian silk running down her thick back, gossiped loudly about one or the other's husband. She recognized them from the two 18-story buildings that completed the square of the concrete jungle. They paused to roll their eyes at her as if she were the husband stealer and then returned to their conversation.

With $37.15—my father's money—nestled deep in the pocket of her Woolworth's jeans, she ordered five pounds of whiting and a box of yellow cornmeal. This act, so simple for most, was for us a serious sin. With the ordering of the fish, she'd broken one of my father's most important rules. "I'm experienced now girl, no longer a virgin," she told me later with an unrecognizable delight in her voice. Above her head a large white sign read **Large Shrimp - $3.99 a pound** in red and she stared at that to avoid watching the fish man work with expert hands to remove fish heads, scales and fins.

"He always was a liar," she'd muttered, as she looked around at the non-frightening boxes of food on the store shelves.

My father had promised us that if we *ever* stepped foot inside of a fish market, on *that day* we would drop dead. We believed him – that's what children do. But whenever he'd made this promise, Kala would wink at me, and suck her teeth like she knew the truth. And apparently she did because she was, standing in the forbidden place, alive and well. She'd actually laughed (which was shocking) when her stomach started growling loudly and the two women from the twin buildings stared at her "real funny like." Billy Kettle, who had begun cleaning his fingernails with a pocketknife, had also looked at her with an uncomfortable sympathy.

"You want cleaned and de-boned?" asked the Korean man behind the counter.

"Yeah," she answered because she thought she should. Her fingers tightened on the money in her pocket; it had given her strength.

"Two dollar extra," the cashier warned.

"Okay," she'd responded, feeling Wonder Woman powerful as he scraped, cleaned and lassoed her fish, then wrapped it in brown paper.

Just then, the two "Building" women, who Kala said were cursing like a couple of backward sailors, opened the fish market door setting off the overhead bell. The sound startled Kala and she turned her head toward it, too fast. For a second, she'd sworn she could see my father's black ghost standing in the doorway. An Arctic chill gathered at the base of her neck then sped down her spine until it reached her bladder. She shivered next to the glass counter, as if a cup of ice had been dumped into her underwear.

"A few drops of pee trickled down my leg," she admitted.

"Ten dollars!" the fish man declared, slapping the package down on the chrome counter.

Jumping back with a yelp, she'd tried unsuccessfully to hide her fear of my daddy's ghost. Billy Kettle, who'd edged closer, acted as if he was going to say to something to her. But the cold look she flashed him, shut him right up.

"The cornmeal," she'd reminded the fish man, trying to recover from the false image of my father.

"Oh cornmeal, right here," the fish man replied with a smile this time, adding the box to a black plastic bag. "You pay eleven ninety-five, please."

Kala counted out 12 dollars that smelled of my father's cheap liquor, and the fish man handed her a nickel in return. In her hurry to get out of the fish market, she tripped and ran right smack into the huge chest of Miss Ida from two doors down on the right.

"Child, what you doing up here?" Miss Ida asked. Kala who has a dry sense of humor, said her nose was flaring like a hungry pig's.

Nobody knew Miss Ida's last name and Kala kept me in stitches talking about how the matching circular scars on her wrists were evidence that she'd escaped from a chain gang. Miss Ida's hard Southern accent, which often made it hard to understand her, strengthened our belief.

Kala spared me no detail as she described the big ugly smile that creased Miss Ida's pudgy face, and how her large bosom heaved up and down threatening to escape the halter top "that she had no business wearing". Ashes fell from the cigarette dangling from her black lips, landing between her breasts.

"I'm buying some fish Miss Ida," Kala told her, biting down on her bottom lip to suppress the part about how *"this was none of her business"*.

"Fish?" Miss Ida yelled. "Girl you know your daddy don't allow no fish in his house!"

Of course Kala knew that—everybody on the block knew it because my father had repeated his childhood story to anyone who would sit still and listen: *"When I was a boy the only thing we ever had to eat was fish," he would slur, taking a long slip from his ever-present can of Schlitz Malt Liquor. "When I came North, I promised myself I wouldn't ever have another fish on my plate again. Never! Wife and kids neither."*

Once, on one of our hungriest days, Brother had muttered, "Well at least you had fish." He lost three of his baby teeth to a backhand, and I had to beg Kala to not get herself killed going after my father.

In answer to Miss Ida's nosiness, Kala suggested that she, "walk on down to our house a little later and put her nose outside the kitchen window and get herself a big whiff of the fish we were having". She tried to maneuver around the woman's massive frame but she had her solidly blocked from moving forward

"Bu-but your father ain't even cold in his grave yet!" Miss Ida stammered.

"He was cold enough while he was alive," Kala whispered. "Look, I have to go Miss Ida." She was finally able to squeeze pass, trying her best to avoid Miss Ida's hard, white feet. Miss Ida had an odor, but standing outside the fish market Kala said it was hardly noticeable. "See you later now," she'd yelled back, moving as fast as her legs could carry her.

When I thought about this later, I imagined a cool wind at Kala's back blowing her toward home, toward us.

Instead of going to the big supermarket, which frightened all of us, Kala bought milk, eggs, bread, a pound of bologna, and a box of Little Debbie Oatmeal Cream Pies at the corner grocery store. The tiny wife of the owner eyed her suspiciously and she told me

27

she felt proud that for once she hadn't had to steal the food.

Walking toward home, toward us, she'd hummed softly under her breath until she heard, "Hey girl, whatcha' doing out on the street? I heard the Man got 'cha!"

Kala stopped, looked up and saw Pinky, a neighborhood boy so named for his bloodshot eyes and extremely light skin. A smart mouth, and punkish in his ways, he was constantly in trouble with the rest of us kids. His long arms spread lanky across a naked pillow in the windowsill. He grinned down at Kala through the gap in his front teeth.

"Shut up stupid!" my sister shot back. She couldn't stand Pinky, even though she felt bad about how everybody treated him like crap.

"I got some grits up here, girl," Pinky taunted. "Why don't you come and get 'em?"

"Why don't you tell your Momma to buy some new shades so you can take your pissy sheet out of the window, fool," she yelled back, unable to resist the jonsing.

"At least the Man wasn't at my front door last night," an embarrass Pinky, finished weakly pulling down his window, and disappearing inside.

Kala told me that she'd felt bad for a second until she remembered that he'd started it - if you started it, you deserved it.

28

The screen door with the missing screen
squeaked when Kala returned, and there we stood,
eight pairs of identical brown eyes, watering with
want. We parted like the Red Sea, staring at her bag-
filled arms with awe, like they were the staffs Moses
and Aaron carried as they freed the Israelites from
Egypt. She bent over so we could touch the bags.
They felt like a miracle.

"How'd you steal a big bottle of milk?" Sonny
asked.

"I didn't have to steal this boy!" she'd replied,
taking time to run her fingers through his thick, curly
hair. "I *bought* it all."

"For us?" Brother asked.

I saw her turn away quick so she wouldn't see
herself in his empty eyes. She told me once that pain
reflected hardest in the eyes of the youngest. "All of
it, every bit."

We would have broken out in a cheer if we knew
was happiness was about; instead we followed her in
our childlike way, quiet and timid, afraid to jump or
make a loud noise like he was still sleeping away the
day upstairs. It was the four of us huddled at the
table, joined together by love, hunger and fear that
gave her the strength to do what she did next.

Only way I can describe what happened is to tell
you about a teacher I had in the third grade, Miss
Body (pronounced Bo-daé) who had a problem with
her hands. All the kids laughed about it, but I never
did because she snuck me bologna and cheese
sandwiches at lunchtime and it wouldn't have been

nice. Because of her hand problem, Miss Body struggled to hold on to things, like paper, chalk and such. Her fingers gnarled and almost curled under each other, so she was slow to do what we could do easily. It took her 10 minutes sometimes to get a math problem on the blackboard, and you just had to wait patiently to get the point.

It was like that when Kala un-wrapped that fish; it looked like it crippled her some.

"We're going to eat real fine today baby. Poppa done gone away baby," she sung softly, her hands shaking as she poured used grease into the cast iron skillet.

We sat silently, our eyes widening with each of her loving movements. She worked as if she were experienced in the art of fish frying, coating each filet with an egg mixture before rubbing them with cornmeal until she was satisfied that they were completely covered by yellow.

When she tossed the first piece into the pan, it splashed hot grease and she jumped back, a crooked line of steam dampening her face. My stomach growled its approval and I smiled. But then she turned, and I read the fear, big in her eyes.

It was the steam that brought on the memory, how she had seen my father last, all bubbled and burnt, wriggling on the floor like a slimy worm trying to get from underfoot. I saw the change when it came, a misty shade slowly rolling down over her eyes, a cementing of her stance. My hands tightened around the edge of the table like a vise.

There it was, his hand running along the nape of her arched neck, hot, liquored breath slowly breezing across her exposed shoulder, along with the steam - that plain unscented steam from the boiling grits she was stirring on the stove. When he slipped his tongue into her ear, promising things a daddy should never promise his own daughter—things he'd promised and delivered so many times before—Kala gave him them grits.

Grits and boiling water flew through the thick, humid air, exploding from the pot with such a force that he landed two feet away. Those grits, salvation from yet another hungry night, stuck to his face like hot white lava, creating thousands of tiny red rivers of flesh and blood.

Kala watched, more fascinated than horrified, as our father danced like the old mothers of the storefront church, wild, without care or reservation. He was like a drunken puppet with his arms and legs flapping up and down. It might have been comical if we weren't so hungry.

He fell after a minute, slipping in his own blood, screaming and screaming and hollering, snatching at her legs, and cursing her name. She stood over him crying and smiling all at the same time, rejoicing and mourning the moment. After a few more minutes his cries died down to a low howl and Kala bent down and emptied his pockets, clutching his beloved money like a newborn on a nipple. He swiped at her and she fell backward onto her butt into the mixture of cooling grits and warm blood. Even in dying he was loud, hollering so long and so hard that my mother came

31

from behind the locked door of the bathroom, her eyes glassy and confused.

"Lord Jesus, what happened?" she screamed, spinning round and round until it made me a bit dizzy.

Kala, who had wrapped us in her arms, didn't answer.

"Run next door girl and call the ambulance people!" my mother shrieked at Kala. But my sister didn't move. She just stared at her with such a cold look that I shivered in her tight grip.

"Did you hear me girl?" my mother demanded. "Go on now, hurry up!"

But the moaning had stopped and his melted eyelids closed before Kala walked slowly toward the backdoor and pulled it open. The neighborhood greeted her with flapping lips and wide eyes as she stared out into a gray evening. The rain had gotten around to stopping, but the smell of wet bricks filled the kitchen.

"Well, one of y'all gonna call the police or something?" Kala asked. "We got a dead man in here."

"Shut up girl, he ain't dead!" my mother screamed, her eyes crazy-looking and her hands digging in his pants pockets for the money that was already gone. Confusion dusted her face.

Miss Ida from two doors down on the right appeared at our house. "Lord, what's done happened?" she asked, pushing her way through the back door to stand over his body. And then she said, "He's dead."

It was a pronouncement. My brothers and I stood around, each of us finding our way back into Kala's arms where we waited together, for what I wasn't sure. My mother refused to believe he was dead until the white policeman with the tall black boots, shaking his head and picking up a piece of the whiskey bottle he'd dropped during the melee, announced it to a room full of onlookers an hour later.

"He's dead."

"Well I said that," Miss Ida from two doors down on the right replied, insulted that her pronouncement hadn't been sufficient.

My mother screamed then, like a wild person, ran and locked herself back in the bathroom. She left the responsibility of giving my father's name and age to the police with Kala, who in turn predicted that we wouldn't see her until morning or" until the needle broke in her arm".

Since she was in charge, Kala ordered us to go to bed. Four sets of bare feet took off up the steps. Somebody, I can't remember now who, tripped but recovered quickly enough. At the top of the stairs, I snuck out of the pack and watched the action from the landing.

The sun was coming up by the time Kala finished mopping up blood and grits and the police had carried my father out in a black plastic bag. For hours, I listened to her crying as she worked. I don't think I'd ever heard her cry before. When finally she lay down *on the secondhand couch he'd found driving his junk truck through the "white folks'" neighborhood, I slipped off to bed wondering if she still had the smell of him filling her nostrils.*

Kala shook her head and came out of the remembrance, though she still looked dazed to me. She fried the whole five pounds of fish then put on a pot of grits. Since this was a special meal, she took down a serving dish that was rumored to belong to a grandmother I'd never known, and piled it high with food. Five ice-cold glasses of milk were poured into cleaned out jelly and mayonnaise jars and placed in front of our empty plates. The high morning sun beamed through the kitchen windows, landing on her glass, turning her white milk to gold.

"In my mind a choir was singing, 'Hal-le-lu-jah, Hallelujah, Hallelu-jahhh,'" she told me a few months later.

With drops of sweat riding her skin like a tick on a dog, she instructed me to open the windows and the backdoor. The pungent fish odor, unfamiliar, yet inviting, drifted out of our kitchen, spreading the smell of our freedom to the concrete jungle.

"Come on now," Kala said with what I thought to be false brevity. "We can eat now."

"But that's fish," Sonny said, his eyes darting toward the door as if he were expecting "him" to come crashing through it. Brother started crying, loudly. Baby joined in on cue.

34

"Hush now. It's alright now," Kala whispered softly, placing a fillet and a serving of grits on each of our plates. She added butter and salt to her own and we followed suit.

"There is nothing to be afraid of any more. It's only breakfast. See, look at me."

With that, she brought the fish to her lips, nibbled a little, then nibbled some more. Fingers greasy, skin glowing, Kala threw her head back and laughed. We waited patiently, each of us desperately hungry, as she savored the crumby feeling of fish on her lips. Most beautiful thing I'd seen in my eleven years that look of accomplishment in her face. She looked at me with a kind of crooked smile, tears swimming in her eyes, and I could see her mind soaring with a sense of rebellion she had never felt before. Understanding flooded me, nearly drowning me in the lesson, as I bit into my fish and feasted upon the shared taste of freedom.

"We going to die," Brother announced, biting into his piece, silly grin on his face.

"But least we eating first," Sonny added, as he pushed Baby's hand away from his plate.

"We ain't gonna do no such a thing," Kala replied, smiling through the tears coating her sweaty cheeks. "No, we're gonna live. For the first time, we're gonna live."

Two Fish

CHAPTER ONE - Aunt Mary

School got started two weeks after those boiling grits. To be honest us little ones were still in shock and couldn't told, if the police had bothered to ask, what happened that night. I expected them to come and take us away, to arrest Kala for what she'd done. I kept imaging her in black and white stripes breaking bricks on the side of a dirt road (my father's favorite black and white movie was "I'm a Fugitive from the Chain Gang"). They never did come and I realized much later, when I had grown older and wiser to the rules of ghetto living, that another dead black man in the projects wasn't worth the paperwork it would take to investigate his death. Apparently the jungle residents agreed because it wasn't three days after he died that I heard that Miss Ida was joking about somebody name Al Green getting the same kind of dance ticket from a girlfriend. We had a mother (even if we didn't see her much), so the welfare and projects people left us alone.

We went back to school in what we had. Kala and my clothes were a bit tighter and the boys' pants were a bit higher from the ankle. We had no money for the Laundromat so Kala hand-washed all our clothes in the bathtub and I helped her hang them out on the nylon clothesline. (Of course our underwear was left in the bathroom to dry out because she said it was indecent to put them outside.) I remember looking forward to using that clothesline as a jump rope when the sidewalks were cooler and packed with kids looking for a breath of fresh air and an end-of-summer moment. But for now, the sun was scorching the red brick of the projects along with our bodies.

As she normally did, Kala sent the boys out to play in the backyard while our school clothes dried. Besides playing "Tag" or pretending to be "Batman and Robin" they were there to make sure our clothes didn't disappear mysteriously among the alleyways of the jungle only to be seen again on the back of a neighbor and/or a junkie wandering through. Sonny, Brother and Baby didn't care much; they would play wherever Kala let them, as long as they got to play. Now that our father was gone, they even laughed some.

At that point, the windfall of groceries was long gone and my stomach growled with its usual hunger and a newer sense of irritation. That irritation came from the loss of my favorite possession, a beat up fake gold medal I'd won in the community center's relay race the previous summer. It had disappeared in the middle of the night along with my mother. Why she'd want that thing I couldn't figure, but Kala said she probably thought it was made of some sellable metal.

"She's gonna be surprised when the pawn shop man hands her a quarter," Kala said with a grin. She stopped smiling when she realized how upset I was about the whole thing, pressing a dollar into my hand to make it up to me.

"What's this for?" I asked my sister, hoping for once she would actually say how she felt about me.

"You go ahead now. Get yourself something. Anything you want to make it all feel better," Kala replied.

My eyes filled with tears and I hugged her real tight even though I knew she hated that kind of display. Then I tried to push the bill back in her hand because I knew we needed it for food or something important.

Kala jumped away from me like I had touched her with a hot iron.

"Keep the dollar," she commanded. "I got a job."

The news stunned me for a minute. "How'd you get a job?" I asked accusingly. "You're too young to get a job."

"I'ma be working with Esther from around the corner and four doors down," she replied, busying herself with making lunch, a can of beans but no hot dogs. "Esther works at night cleaning those big buildings downtown and I'm gonna help her out."

I didn't try to change Kala's mind because I know once it's made, it's as tight as a sheet on a fresh-made bed. In fact, the plan was that she was going to start the very next night, at 10. If I was frightened— and to be truthful I can't remember for sure because it's been so many years—I didn't display it. I only remember looking out at the boys charging crazily at each other with cardboard swords and newspaper hats, wishing I was right out there in the middle of their imaginary war where the wounds didn't bleed red.

I got my period the third day after the first day of school. This wasn't some great event. Fifth grade was full of little girls getting a visit from their famed, never previously seen Aunt Mary. But I was probably the only one who had belted Kotex in her backpack and knew exactly what to do with them when the old lady finally came to visit me. Way before my period started, Kala and I had spent an hour practicing how to use the darn things. She checked my school bag every morning to make sure that I hadn't taken them out and tossed them under the bed or something. Kala didn't want what happened to her when Aunt Mary came to visit for the first time to happen to me.

"It was nothing to be proud of or happy about. More a horror, how it all went down," is how she explained it to me. See, he had been at her for three years already, and she was only 11 then. Night before her "Aunt Mary" came to visit, he climbed into the bed we shared, and had her screaming, fighting and kicking 'til he looked over at me and she saw what he was thinking in his eyes. Then she just lay real still and let him do it. She told me to get in the closet, but I was so scared of that closed in space I scurried under the bed with the water bugs and such, and covered my ears so I couldn't hear a thing. But that squeaking, it found a way through the cracks of my fingers, and the mattress weighed down so far it nearly touched my back.

The next morning her lips were busted up pretty good and one eye was near 'bout closed, but my mother took one look at her and sent her to school. "Can't stand to look at you," is what I remember she said.

Aunt Mary came during science, her third class of the day, while they were cutting up pieces of frogs— not whole frogs mind you, just pieces 'cause the poor things had already been dissected by the kids who had science for their first and second class. "Sad when a school can't afford to give a child their own frog to slice up," she'd added, shaking her head.

Her science partner was a boy we called Boogie (no need to explain why). Boogie's mother, Miss Bertha, is also the lunchroom lady so anybody who got close with him normally got a better lunch than the others. Only problem with Boogie is that he liked to *play too much*. This day, he threw a piece of frog leg at Kala's good eye. She screamed, Boogie ducked down to keep from taking the punch she was directing at his face, and that's why he was the one who saw that Aunt Mary had arrived in a silent river of red. Well Boogie, who's too dark to blush, got to yelling and pointing so much that the entire class turned to look. Because of her eye and busted lip, Mr. Epstein, the science teacher (but he also taught gym), thought Kala might have something called internal bleeding so he took off his plaid jacket and rushed her to the nurse, who announced to him and all the people standing around being nosey, "The girl has simply started her period."

Realizing that no one was gonna die or at least rushed off in an ambulance, the crowd melted away and the school nurse explained to her that all women have a distant relative who comes to stay with them for about 50 years or so, though she only comes out of her room to speak to you once a month. Right after that, not knowing for sure when Aunt Mary would visit with me Kala stuffed a Kotex and a belt in my bag and made me keep it there. I didn't matter that my flow didn't start until four years later.

So when I told her that afternoon, the third day after the first day of school, that Aunt Mary had finally arrived, she burst into tears and hugged me tight. She did that a lot after he was gone. She kept mumbling over and over again, "He didn't get you before you became a woman. He didn't get you." At

9, I wasn't sure what that meant, but I got it real clear now. That makes me love her even harder.

CHAPTER TWO - The Uncle Parade

With the death of our father and the intermittent visits of our mother, Kala Ann (her middle name is the same as my mother's so you know she hates it) took control of the house. She ordered us about like an army sergeant insisting that we do our chores and homework before any play or free time. We struggled to adjust to the sound of our laughter, our bickering, and western movies, when the television felt like working. She did the best she could and we went to bed with full bellies each night. It wasn't that we ate better, but we did eat more. Before our father danced in those grits, there were plenty of nights of empty bowls and clean spoons. Now our bowls were full of something every night: soup, oatmeal, tuna casserole—just about anything she could find and fix to fill us up. I was relieved when school started and we had access to free breakfast and lunch again 'cause it took some of the fear out of her eyes. But she still worried all the time, still had a need to since my mother was lurking about, a skeleton with big red eyes. She was one of the things that stayed the same. Her drug habit didn't get better because her husband no longer supported it. It actually intensified, becoming more dangerous for her offspring.

Took only about a month after my father died, before my mother started bringing home the men.

The first one was Uncle Zackary. Had two big buckteeth and one wandering eye, but at least he kept it on her and not us. He showed up with a bucket of chicken and a liter of whiskey, making himself right at home on our little broken down couch. Kala was livid, but what could she do? What could anybody do but shake their head and wag a tongue about the shame of it. Mr. Zachary came around nightly for about two weeks, 'til he got his Social Security check and my mother robbed him while he was passed out in a drunken stupor on our living room floor. I felt sorry for him crying and all, snot running down his nose and tears running crooked out of his bad eye, but Kala said, "He got what was coming his way. He should have known that larva wasn't ever gonna be no butterfly." Now this was right in the middle of her helping me with a caterpillar project, so I knew just what she was talking about.

The second one of 'em wasn't long in coming. Uncle Willie, as we were forced to call him, looked just like my mother, walking death. He was always peering at everything, licking his white lips and blinking real fast "just like a liar," Kala would say. I never did figure out why he kept pulling the kitchen drawers open or checking under the bathroom sink like he was expecting a dollar bill to jump out or something. I asked him once just 'cause it was getting on my nerves, but he never replied; he just tried to stare me down. When he figured out that we didn't have nothin' to steal, which would have taken a sane man only a minute, he moved on.

Uncle Arnold, Uncle Donald and Uncle Doug followed - a sad array of sad men looking for Lord knows what in my mother. It was a pitiful parade, but Kala said it wouldn't last. She was right. It stopped just as suddenly as it started when the police got a tip that my mother was the one who broke into Kresge's and stole a case of transistor radios. She was released from jail a month later and by that time Kala had the locks changed and had taught me how to seal the windows shut at night with wood planks we found in abandoned houses.

CHAPTER THREE – The Two Rule Rule

We lived by two rules designed and incorporated specifically for the concrete jungle. They were never to be broken. The first one: Always be suspicious of someone *who's not* from our neighborhood. The second: Always be suspicious of someone who *is* from our neighborhood. See Kala said if we simply lived by these two rules we would always be safe. "Not fed, not warm, not even happy, but safe."

The change from summer to fall was measured not by the falling of orange, gold and brown, but by how slowly our ice cream cones melted as we sat on the front stoop. We drifted into a routine of school, play, dinner and bed, where the lives of *The Brady Bunch* kids had more importance than our own. Wet cool breezes pushed potato chip bags and soda cans up and down from house to house, and we fought the never-ending battle of keeping the little patch of grass we called a lawn clean. By six o'clock the streets were pitch black on starless nights, shades pulled down, living room and kitchen lights turned on, illuminating the long block from the inside out. Sweaters were retrieved from the top of the closet and cans of soup or bowls of oatmeal were heated for dinner. When night fell, sometimes so quickly that we had to run to beat it home, we traded cement for linoleum, taking seats on the cool floor to touch hands in a fast paced game of "Mary Mack" or a slower paced "Patty Cake" if we were entertaining Baby.

One such fall evening, I stared out of the window at Miss Josie Kitt (yes her real name) who lived across the street, four doors from the barbershop where Mr. Turner, the half-blind barber cut the hair of the boys in the neighborhood. Miss Josie was screaming and yelling at some adversary from her top step. Since her apartment building was across from the concrete jungle that proximity meant she inherited our rules, regulations and problems.

A group of kids, two of which I recognized from my 4th grade class at Hartranft Elementary, paused long enough to throw a few cans at her and received a good drunken cussing out before moving on. From the second floor Miss Josie's only daughter, a tall awkward thing of a girl, Josette (poor thing had the misfortune to be permanently identified with her mother) stuck her head in and out of the window as if she was trying to decide how to coax her mother inside. I liked Josette but she was too shy to hold on to a friendship with me or anyone else. (Naturally I was shocked to see her pregnant three years later by Antoine Wilson, the local basketball star.)

With the paint-coated steel windowsill cutting into the back of my arms and the streetlights popping on and off with a sick buzz, I smiled as the show wound down. Miss Josie's clear liquor bottle was turned upside down, indicating that she was dry and soon the comedy would be over for the evening.

But things didn't end before a car quietly approached - its black body and tinted windows blending into the dusk.

"Whatcha' doing 'round here white man?" Miss Josie said, her sloppy voice carried by the fall wind. "I say whatcha' doing 'round here? Looking for a woman?"

I would have missed that car altogether if not for Miss Josie. But now I stared at it with great interest, straining my eyes to get a glimpse of the driver. Suddenly, as if he knew that I was watching, he pulled off with a loud screech leaving a thick sulfur-smelling cloud of smoke behind. Kala called me for something and I forgot all about the car and the mystery driver— until the next week when again he rolled through our jungle.

He came several times after that first night when Miss Josie had cussed him out. We were naturally suspicious, and just a little bit shocked. Creeping by slowly, white lights shining so bright they blinded you for a few seconds when they hit you directly in the face, he would peer out of the half-open tinted windows always hiding everything but his eyes and baldhead. To me, his eyes looked dead black, like the polished steel of his car. When Kala finally saw him for the first time, she said, "We don't ever want to get close enough to see the real color of those eyes."

Wasn't nothing we could do but look, but his presence caused a stir in the neighborhood. Mothers stared at the man with disdain then screamed out the names of their children or pulled them tighter if they happened to be within an arm's reach.

"June bug, where are you boy?"

"Roberta, you better come on in now!"

"Harold, don't make me call for you again!"

It was music to my ears that lullaby of hard love and caring. We all showed our disapproval, but he kept coming. And since we were kids and kids do stupid things, we took to throwing rocks at his car and daring him to get out and chase us. He never did though. He just kept riding by, glassy look in those black eyes as he stared at us like we were in the circus and he was the ringmaster.

Halloween came and went, and that car came by three Saturday nights in a row. On the Saturday he didn't show up, my brothers and I argued about where he had gone, but of course nobody could figure it out. Sonny said he was Captain Kirk from *Star Trek*, "going where no man had gone before "to discover unexplored worlds".

A month later, the truth of what he really was would be revealed and intersect with our lives like one

49

of those nightmares while you're awake. By this time, school had descended upon us like a heavy hand. Kala had been a straight "A" student since kindergarten and expected the same from us, although only Sonny ever seemed to meet the mark.

By late fall, we were locked firmly at the kitchen table, buried under composition books and half of an encyclopedia set that my mother in her sober days (which I don't remember mind you) had purchased from a passing book dealer. Kala said she bought them 'cause the rest of the neighbors hadn't. But it remained at a half a set because her heroin habit won over education midway through the purchase agreement. If we had a report to write, Kala said the trick was to pick a topic that ran from the letters A to K and we would be okay. Since I loved zebras, I found this a particularly irritating thing to do. But Kala, in her first year at Kensington High School for Girls, always found a way to keep up her schoolwork, housework and night work.

Watching Kala stir a pot of what we called Poor Man's stew (hotdogs, pork and beans, and onions), flip through the pages of her biology text book, and yell at Brother to finish his paper on his hero, Muhammad Ali, I was amazed by her ability to pay attention to everyone except herself. In those moments sitting at the kitchen table, I wished desperately for her to take notice of herself, to realize how much she offered to the world and just take the time to be noticed. I had no idea that in only a few short weeks, my dream for her would come true or that it would again be tied to fish.

When Kala was invited by her school's science club to join them on an "exploration" to the Atlantic Ocean, I knew this was a special opportunity. But she refused to go. She didn't want to leave us, not even for a day. So I talked to Miss Mickins from next door, who was more a mother to us than our own, and she convinced Kala to accept the offer.

The morning of the trip, after giving Miss Mickins a crumpled $5.00 bill to see us in the house by 6:00, and getting my sworn promise to give the boys sardine sandwiches and put them to bed that night, she left the house looking back every few steps as if we were going to disappear.

She was excited about the trip, though she'd rather be whipped naked with a switch in front of the entire neighborhood than admit to it. I was happy about her chance, but when she left that morning with excitement and a pile of fear in her beautiful brown eyes, I just about cried. The sun was hanging high above ribbons of white clouds, and Miss Mickins told her that it was a glorious morning and she should have a wonderful time.

Much later, after that sun had long been down and night had crept upon the jungle, she told me all about that trip.

Said the smell hit her first, even before they collected their things and piled off the bus. It reminded her of the fish we'd eaten the day after my father died, and the freedom we felt. Standing in the sun, the city only an hour and a half away, worry peeled slowly from her browning skin.

51

"Okay I want everyone to listen carefully to these instructions. We are going to be pulling out from this very stop at exactly 5:00 P.M.," announced the science teacher. "Those of you who have volunteered for specimen collection can follow me and we will spend an hour..."

Kala missed the rest of his directions because she was staring past him, at the white crashing waves and brownish-white sand ahead.

She headed towards the water alone. She wasn't supposed to get in just yet, especially in her blue jeans and such, but excitement flooded her chest. She headed for the water, the feel of the waves crashing deep inside of her. Her feet sunk into the thick sand, and she stopped, surprised by the affect. Around her, kids were ripping off sneakers and socks and she followed suit. Her toes curled upon the granules.

"It felt like grits," she reported. "But that sand was almost like heaven, weightless, but wholly solid, and for just that moment, little sister, I almost forgave your mother. Almost."

It was a magical moment for Kala. She'd savored it, tasted it, and let it freeze her brain like a Popsicle eaten too quickly. When her bare feet finally touched the chilly, sandy water, she jumped back, surprised by the power of the foamy waves first rushing towards her then receding. Even at the water's edge she could feel the force of the endless ocean. Emboldened by her first steps, she walked into the water a second time. She didn't understand the ocean's power until the waves reached her waist and knocked her about in their greenish depth. She stood up, sputtering and spitting out the salty water, her eyes burning with joy.

I still haven't stopped considering the next thing that happened, even after all of these years. Kala said that right while she was standing in it, the ocean turned into a sea of endless whiskey, strong and dizzying. It dragged her further and further into its midst and she flung her arms wildly trying to escape the force. Then she heard his voice, my father's voice, hoarse and scratchy.

"Come 'ere girl. Got somethin' to show yah."

Something started dragging her under, sucking the breath from lungs, like jealous cats do to babies when they're left unattended. Kala realized that it was him coming to exact his revenge. She fought hard, kicking and screaming, but he was winning like he always did.

Kala landed hard on the ocean floor, pinned by some invisible weight. Her eyes flew open and that's when she saw them: Two golden fish, long as her arms with huge translucent eyes that allowed her to see the world straight through them to us playing jacks on our front step. "Go home," one of them ordered.

Kala stood up and walked right out of that ocean, clothes dripping salt water and seaweed on the sand. I didn't bother to tell her that Miss Mickins had bought us a brand new pack of jacks and we were out playing on the step waiting for her to come home. I figured she already knew from the two fish who saved her life.

When Kala got home, she felt the wrong before she saw it. As she later told me, it greeted her at the front door, like a sheet of ice chilling her blood. It was the quiet, the blackness and the heavy scent of cologne that was out of place in our home. Where was the blue haze emanating from the secondhand television set? Where was the buzz of expectancy? Where were we?

"Brother? Sonny? Where are you?" she'd shouted, as the salt-water taffy and shells she'd brought back for us slipped from her hands. "Come out now, stop playing!" But she knew we weren't playing a game. We didn't play hide and go seek. We had too many real boogey men to fear.

Always brave beyond her years, she'd tiptoed up the steps, not knowing what to expect and wishing she'd grabbed some kind of weapon on her way up. I smelled her before I actually saw her. Smelled like salt and sea and new things. I was standing in the dark outside my mother's bedroom, my ear pressed hard against the door.

Kala raised a finger to my trembling lips and whispered, "What's wrong?" Her clothes still damp and sticky from salt and sand made me think of my father. I told her then how my mother had come home, maybe 30 minutes before, with a strange white man who didn't belong to our concrete jungle.   I'd watched her take him to the room Brother, Sonny and Baby shared. Through a crack in our bedroom door, in the dim light hanging from the hallway ceiling, I saw their lips whispering and their heads together real tight. I watched my mother go into the boys' room, and come out with Baby in her arms looking up at her with a sleepy smile. She and that man took Baby to her bedroom. After hearing the click of the lock, I came out and put my ear to the door.

Even in the soft yellowish light of the hallway, I saw Kala's brown skin blanch. "Go get me the screw driver out the kitchen closet," she ordered, and I ran fast as I could to retrieve it. When I returned, she snatched it from me and shoved me hard into our bedroom. Told me, "Don't you come out, no matter what you hear? You hear?" I nodded as she pulled the door shut and waited. My stomach tied in knots as muffled sounds, strange sounds, sick-sounding sounds, drifted beneath our bedroom door.

To this day I promise you, I don't know what happened in that room, but 30 minutes later I heard the sound of footsteps, heavy steps, and low cussing. Then there was bathwater running and the sweet sound of her voice as she crooned a song to Baby. I waited until I felt her weight and heard the squeaking of our shared bed before I asked, "Tell me about the beach, please." And she did until I fell asleep in her arms.

CHAPTER FOUR -Baby

My mother didn't come back for a week, not out of shame for her behavior, but out of fear that Kala would kill her. The white man never came back at all. Even before this incident, I had noticed the way my mother looked at my sister. Since my father died, she'd been eyeing her oldest with the wariness of a tomcat making his way through the trashcan of a dog owner. I think she expected her to strike at her any moment. Truth is I thought Kala would too. Funny thing was she never did.

Instead, there was a new sadness about her that none of us could force out, not even Baby, who had recovered the joys of childhood quicker than the rest of us. Kala watched him like a hawk, but he didn't seem to be any worse for the wear after what happened that night.

When Baby was born we didn't get him right away. Doctors wouldn't let him come home with my mother and the monster (my word not Kala's) because he was born with the same sickness that invaded my mother's body. Three or four months passed before the social worker lady came over with him. We knew something significant was about to happen because my parents had been nice that week and, more importantly, sober.

It wasn't even a minute after the door barely missed the social worker's flowing blue skirt with the sunflowers planted on it before Baby belonged to Kala. He was the most beautiful boy, with brown robust cheeks and shiny black eyes that didn't quite seem to focus. He cried a lot from some invisible aches and pains, would only quiet down for her.

It took six months for us to realize that he wasn't like us, probably wasn't never gonna be. But Kala saw different. At 2, when he still didn't walk, she carried him on her bony hip everywhere she went. Baby would have slept with us, but my father wasn't having it. "He didn't want Baby in between him and me," she explained, when I asked her why. So Baby was put in bed with Sonny and Brother who cried and complained almost every morning that he had peed on them again.

Kala, determined that Baby would walk, worked with him until finally one day he did. That was one of the proudest days of her life, the day Baby took his first steps. He even learned to run around pretty good, and although he still couldn't talk without slurring his words he always had a dopey little grin on his face that made you want to hug him. I watched her watching him and knew in my heart that she was his true mother, whether he'd come from her body or not.

About two weeks after the incident with the white man in our house, Baby fell sick with a burning fever that left his lips cracked and bleeding. Kala wrapped him tight in the blanket from our bed, boarded the trolley and then the bus, and took him to St. Christopher's Hospital for Children at 4th and Lehigh. They called it pneumonia.

A new word in my vocabulary that I'd learned from Kala, who had added that word to hers as soon as the doctors named it. The doctors wanted my mother there. Kala didn't, but they refused to deal with her. Said they had to see my mother or they would call the welfare people. Kala tried to take Baby out of there but they wouldn't let her. She told me all of this when she came home, tired and weary. While she was gone, I worried myself sick about her and Baby.

Sonny was crying, and Brother mumbled something then locked himself away (he did that a lot now). I ran to the dictionary to look up pneumonia, its cause and cure. After everyone was given large doses of this horrible cod liver oil that left our stomachs in knots and tied us to the toilet for the day, Kala began her search for my mother.

As much as Kala hated my mother, I think somewhere deep down inside she loved her too. Why else would she keep track of her whereabouts and have any inclination of where to begin her search for her? I think there was some love, just some small inkling of it wrapped in an old memory, but after that day whatever may have remained died for sure.

Kala's first step was Billy Kettle, the Vietnam vet. He had one of the most brilliant minds ever created, but he'd come home with a vicious heroin addiction. At the safe house for junkies he ran, Billy only had one rule (we all had rules). "Don't bring no shit to my door and I won't bring no shit down on you."

Everybody knew Billy Kettle still had a large rifle he'd brought home with him from the war 'cause he liked to shoot it off every Fourth of July in his own personal salute: "God Bless America, but The Man, he ain't shit." I once asked Kala what Billy meant by that and she said, "Billy did right by the war, but the war didn't do right by him." To that I replied, "How can war do right by anybody?" She just looked at me funny, like I was stupid for not understanding that open-ended statement (as you can tell, I'm not), which made me mad, but not mad enough to tell her so.

Anyway, my mother and Billy Kettle were old friends. Once, after Billy sent her home with an abrupt, "Take care of your kids!" she told us about how he had asked to marry her before she married my father. I can't tell you how much I wish she'd taken him up on that offer. Clearly he still had a little crush on her—he must have, 'cause he kept letting her back in to do her "stuff" even when he put others out permanently.

When Kala arrived at Billy Kettle's apartment, number 802 on the eighth floor of Building Number One, the elevator, more broken than running, was actually working. This saved her from taking the exit stairway full of urine and *"other things I don't want to think about."*

"You seen her?" Kala asked Billy, with more grit than necessary.

She said he looked her up and down with a kinda' proud smile, taking her attitude 'cause my mother had lied to him once and said she might be his. Kala had heard her bragging to one of her girlfriends that Billy would do anything for her because they use to date when my father took long truck hauling trips. Still, anybody that could count to 20 knew that Kala couldn't be Billy's because Kala looked just like my father. Still, Billy had a soft spot for her.

"Not in a couple days," he answered, leaning heavy on his handmade wood carved African cane the old dudes like him had started to carry. "She got in an argument with one of my customers, and I couldn't have that up in here."

"Thanks," Kala mumbled, pressing the down button for the elevator. Billy Kettle touched her arm and she nearly jumped out of her skin and screamed, "Get off of me!"

She told me that he looked shocked and a little hurt.

"Sorry girl. Real sorry. Didn't mean nothin'." The elevator came just then, loaded with folks, but she squeezed in among the masses and headed toward her second stop, which wasn't so nice.

Three blocks away from the jungle, on Colorado Street, there's a three-story house closer to falling down than standing. A flophouse, Kala called it, a place where junkies go to buy and then shoot up their drugs. It's on a small one-way street. On either side there are abandoned houses where, according to Kala, *the junkies work to support their stinking habit."*

Word was that nobody but junkies should ever go there 'cause you could be murdered, or worse. (I still don't know what is worse than being murdered, and I don't want to find out.)

The flophouse and adjoining buildings are run by whichever gang has control of the block at that time. A gang had to fight for the right to run the drug business, and control the money. "Killing each other for the right to kill us," Kala said once after a boy who was in her ninth grade class was gunned down on his way home.

The Ministers were a new gang that recruited members between the ages 10 to 35. They chose that name because they said they provided for the needs of the people. The Ministers controlled Colorado Street, a dead place where the few remaining neighbors hid behind gated windows and doors, peeped out of cracked shades and rarely called the police who rarely bothered to come.

With muscles tight and bulky, the Ministers were ready to pounce on anybody or anything that moved. On the rooftop of two of the crumbling buildings they ran, the glint of their handguns bounced off the sun, reflecting down to the street to blind Kala for a moment. The smell of feces and urine permeated the air, and she could hear dogs barking in the distance. As Kala proceeded up the block, none of the gang members stopped her. But somebody called out "fresh bait!" She could feel their eyes burning into her flesh. She said she felt like she'd walked a mile to get to the middle of the block and she'd broken out in a drenching sweat as she approached the house that served as the gang's headquarters. Four Ministers stood up, waiting patiently for her arrival.

"You looking?" asked a kid about 12 years old. A light misty rain began to fall, dampening her face and causing her to shiver a bit.

"Gotta' find somebody," she'd said boldly. "Her boy is sick in the hospital." They laughed, bending over with stomach cramps, and wiping tears from the corners of their eyes.

"That's crazy! You're crazy! Ain't nobody here that cares girl. You know that," said the first boy. In his face, Kala saw Brother and that scared her into silence for a moment. She started to turn around, but then she remembered Baby all alone in the hospital.

"I just want to look, that's all."

"That's gonna cost you girl," the tallest of the group interjected stepping forward. "Open your shirt. Let me see what you got."

"No," she'd whispered looking around, suddenly realizing the danger. "I got five dollars. Only need to look around for the boy's momma."

She saw the look in their eyes and knew what was coming. She turned to run, but two of them had her before she got two steps away, grips like iron burned into her upper arms. She kicked and wailed, and they laughed telling her, "Scream all you want. Ain't nobody coming to help you!"

Kala said she knew that was true, which broke my heart. I wanted her to stop then, not tell any more of this story because my stomach was cramping like Aunt Mary was visiting when she had packed up and left last week. But her eyes were so blank that I couldn't stop listening. I grabbed her hands 'cause they were shaking with the telling and I needed to do something, anything, to help her.

"They dragged me in that flophouse like I was a bag of trash, bumping my head and such." (She did have a big knot on the back of her head.) "They threw me on a naked floor and I knew right then and there I was gonna have to kill somebody 'cause I couldn't let them do it to me, not again, not ever again."

I started crying, wiping my tears with the back of my hands, then took hers again even though they were slippery.

"The little one who looks like Brother, he drops his pants 'cause they make him, and I can see why he was fronting and didn't want to, cause the boy got on Underoos. *Underoos*! Can you believe that?"

At that moment, I smiled, imagining Batman and Robin hanging out on the butt of a gang member.

"They forgot about me for a second. They were laughing so hard that I ran for the door. Had it open too, and was getting out of there when the tall one chokes me up." No doubt he would have killed her too, choked the life right out of her if the door hadn't opened and if two of the older gang members hadn't strolled through it.

"What's up Young Bucks?" said a man with salt and pepper hair. The other one, a fat dude that could have been a male Miss Ida, gave the group of them a menacing look. He had a mustache and a full beard that had a long scar running straight through from the right to the left side. Kala said just looking at him terrified her.

"Nothin'. This girl wants something for nothin', is all. We're teaching her a lesson."

"I just wanted to look around," Kala cried out in her defense. "Just need to find a sick boy's momma!"

Everything went dead silent and she knew her life was in the next words that came out of Salt and Pepper's mouth.

63

"All right, you take a look and then don't ever come back here," the leader said. Then, turning to the tallest of the young gang members, he commanded, "Show her the house and then get your butt back here." The tall boy grabbed Kala's arm viciously and dragged her to a house two doors down.

It was black inside even though the sun hung fat and pregnant in the late-day sky. The windows were boarded up, not to keep people out but to keep them from looking within. "See junkies, they don't like light, or openness of any kind, mirrors even," Kala told me with a confidence that made me believe her. "They're sort of like vampires; they don't want to see themselves, or each other. It took me longer than a minute to adjust to the dark, and I promise you, there will be nights when I wish I hadn't."

They were everywhere, living skeletons, walking, talking, half-dead corpses, staring at her with wet, hungry eyes. Seemed like it was hundreds, nodding, shooting needles in their arms, and digging into their skin with ragged, dirty fingernails.

"I wanted to vomit from the stink and the heartbreak," Kala sadly noted.

Pinky's sister Rita sat in one of the crowded rooms, her back up against a peeling wall with some Puerto Rican guy Kala didn't recognize. Their shoulders leaning against each other's, their heads hung low toward their laps, they never looked up. She'd looked around real good, lifting up people, kicking rats and trash out of her path. She didn't find my mother there and I silently thanked God, both for bringing Kala back, and for her lack of success. Some things it's just better not to know.

It was on her way home, exhausted and scared, worried sick about Baby and us too, that she stumbled upon my mother. "It was more like I tripped on the unleveled sidewalk along York between 10th and 11th streets, and found myself looking at the brown circle birthmark on the back of her neck through the backseat window of Mr. Delgado's purple and gold Lincoln Continental." I could see that she didn't want to tell me the part about what my mother and the Puerto Rican storeowner were doing. But it was the truth and I guess she figured I better know it in case I happened to stumble past it in the future. They weren't even two blocks from his home, right in front of the Rock Solid Non-Denominational Store Front Church, where Preacher Peifoy was pastor.

Kala found herself sitting on the steps of the church just looking at that car, Mr. Delgado yelling out something in Spanish, and my mother's bobble head, bobbling. The doors of the church opened suddenly, surprising her, and the women coming out. She stood and turned to move out of the way of the "saints," and right there on the door, the sunlight turning them into silver liquid, were two beat up looking steel fish.

"They saw into my soul, I know it," she exclaimed. "I knew it was those fish, that it was God in that church who helped me to find her."

"Honey can we help you?" asked an elderly lady dressed in white from head to toe.

"No ma'am. I was looking for my brother's mother but I think God just led me to her."

"Well, praise God."

"From whom all blessings flow," two other women, also in white, chimed in.

"Well where is she child?"

"Right over there, in Mr. Delgado's car, giving him a blow job."

Kala and I burst into laughter when she told me this part. Not out of disrespect, but just because it was funny, the way their faces looked at her words.

The Delgados were one of the only Puerto Rican families in the neighborhood and they owned a small corner store a block away from our house. Mr. Delgado ran the store with his two teenage sons. Their only daughter was Kala's age and she only helped out when absolutely necessary. Mrs. Delgado was only seen in the store during school hours and rarely on weekends. They lived in a large apartment above the store that was decorated with tall, colorful candles decorated with pictures of Jesus and Mary. This was all according to Miss Lydia, Pinky's mother, from 12 houses down. She was pretty friendly with the Delgados since she was half Mexican and spoke Spanish.

"Excuse me now, I gotta' go get her to the hospital," Kala told the saints. "But I'll be coming back on Sunday with my brothers and sister if that's okay."

66

They nodded silently as she backed up smiling at them until she reached the car.

"Hey, hey!" she screamed banging on the car window. "Your boy is sick and you need to go to the hospital!" Poor Mr. Delgado was so shocked that he jumped up and hit his head on the ceiling and knocked my mother's head into the passenger backseat window. Kala kept banging against the glass as he rushed to pull up his pants and until my mother finally stepped out of the car screaming and cussing about her money."

"Baby's in the hospital. It's Pneumonia."

"Whatcha want me do about it?" my mother asked.

"You're going to the hospital to sign the papers so they can treat him. They're going to call Social Services if you don't come," Kala said with disgust. "And Mr. Delgado over there is going to drive us. *Right now.*"

The short stubby man with the receding hairline was so happy not to hear Mrs. Delgado's name come out of Kala's mouth that he nodded his head in agreement. His light brown skin reddened to a purple hue as the ladies who'd come out of the church shook their heads back and forth and twisted their lips in his direction.

"I ain't going nowhere. I need my money," my mother said in the desperate voice of a junkie. Kala later said she couldn't help comparing the women all dressed in white, faces full of concern, to the ashy, heroin-sick woman wiping her lips with the back of her hand.

"How much are you worth now?" Kala asked,

"Twenty dollars," my mother lied.

"Pay her Mr. Delgado," Kala said climbing into the backseat of his car.   It was warm and kinda sticky. Her mother climbed in beside her. "Let's go."

It had taken her three precious hours to find my mother and by the time Mr. Delgado's Lincoln pulled into the emergency room driveway, the afternoon was drifting away behind the crumbling buildings of North Philly. My mother, in a nod, sat quietly. Mr. Delgado placed a crisp $20 bill on the seat beside Kala. He was unable to look her in the eye.

"We need some groceries," she said to him.

"I'm sorry about this," he replied, in his heavy accent. "I'll bring some tomorrow."

"That will be fine," she said, forcing a smile that I'm sure never quite met her eyes.

Mr. Delgado helped Kala lift my mother out of the car and place her not so gently into a hospital wheelchair that must have been left by a previous patient. Somehow the front desk got her signature on the necessary forms and we were saved once again from DHS (the Department of Human Services). Baby came home after a week in St. Christopher's and my mother disappeared again into the places where the walking skeletons wander. With the help of Mr. Delgado's weekly grocery donation, we did eat a little better so I just couldn't find it in my heart to be mad at him.

CHAPTER FIVE - Getting Saved

After Kala spotted those two fish on the doors of Rock Solid Non-Denominational Store Front Church where Preacher Peifoy was the Pastor, we started attending morning services. As non-churchgoers we went with great trepidation and curiosity. Kala actually dragged Brother kicking and screaming by both hands since he was afraid all of his sins would cause the church to blow up when he walked through the doors.

It was a big place to us, though it was probably considered small to other churches. I had to push Sonny along the aisle because he kept staring crazily at the colored pictures of Jesus, Mary and the Disciples hanging along the walls. Baby started clapping with the music coming from the front and every head and set of eyes turned toward us and remained there. I felt like one of those little lambs at the petting zoo as Kala marched us straight down the red carpet that separated the 60 or so folding chairs. Kala didn't stop 'til she got to the third row, right behind the women in white, who now wore wide hats to match their outfits.

In the front, a robe-less choir was singing a song I had never heard before. The leader looked a little like Donna Summers, long hair and all, except her hair was white as December snow. Her gold polyester three-piece suit was shining under the bright church lights. With a curved cane extending from his arm, an old man began to dance to the beat of drums, piano and guitar. As the tempo picked up, his feet moved faster and faster and I held my breath thinking he would fall to the floor at any moment. But his dance—well known and ancient—continued with no incidents.

I began to feel a heat running down the middle of my back. My foot tapped without permission. In unison, bodies rose around me, hands clapping, holy words flying from spittle-filled mouths as bodies spun and spun around in circles. "The Spirit is here! The Spirit is here!" someone, unseen in the back of the church, yelled. There was Kala, on her feet and her body swaying as if it knew the secret language spoken by the church members. Brother, previously slouched over in his chair, sat up at attention, his interest caught and held by the moment. A look of fear danced across his face, his almond shaped eyes filled up with tears as if this was the moment when he would be "struck down" for his sins.

Sonny clapped out of beat, and Baby jumped up and down, some secret joy filling his heart.

One of the men, Deacon Brown I heard someone call him after service, passed around a gold plate that the members filled with dollars. After about a half hour Pastor Peifoy took his place in from of a podium and began to talk. He spoke for about another hour and I struggled to understand what he was saying, which was hard since I kept nodding off.

"See the little boy who came to hear Jesus, he wasn't thinking he would have to feed five thousand people, but Jesus he knew, he knew."

Whispering in Sonny's ear, I asked him how one boy could possibly do that. He giggled and made Kala look at us like we were horrible.

"No he could have just kept quiet when our Savior asked if anybody had food. But no, no, that boy stood up with faith and offered what little he had and Jesus was able to feed all the folks who came out that day. That's the way we gotta' be saints. We have to feed our neighbors and God will keep feeding us."

The church members started agreeing with him about what he was saying, nodding their heads and waving white handkerchiefs in the air.

"Amen, Pastor!"

"Sure you right. Preach, sir."

Frightened by the entire service, I thought to myself right then, *if this is the way to Heaven I might just take the El the other way.* Then I felt guilty and asked Jesus to forgive me for my ignorance.

When Pastor Peifoy finally finished his message, he asked if anybody wanted to come on up and get saved. I was shocked when Kala and Sonny jumped up from their folding chairs and walked up to the altar. I didn't know what to do, so I followed.

Thirty minutes later, my knees screaming in pain from the kneeling on the hardwood floor, I threw my head back and yelled out as loud as I could, "Praise the Lord, I'm saved!"

With that, church was over and I got out of there as fast as I could maneuver through the crowd of

71

people waiting to congratulate us. Brother woke up just in time to leave. He beat me out the door, his shirt flapping in the early October winds.

CHAPTER SIX - Bread and Steel

Winter blew in with colder breezes and longer shadows. Miss Mickins went in the hospital for a week and Kala took turns helping her girls cook dinner. I felt real sorry for all those kids who sat by the front window looking for their momma. It gave me some peace to know that somebody had a momma who was worth the looking for.

Noodle, the oldest boy who everybody said had robbed a bank on the Avenue, snuck in and out to watch out for his brothers and sisters, but it was still sad with Miss Mickins away. Baby was almost completely recovered although he still looked a little weak to me.

"That boy is strong as an ox," Kala would say when I would ask about his health. "Strong as an ox." But I saw the worry in her big brown eyes and knew I needed to pay closer attention. I was zooming toward the teen years and struggling with the changes in my body and my thinking. My mouth got smarter and cleaner as she made me wash it out with soap a few times for cussing at Brother when he took something of mine. Brother did that a lot, messed with other people stuff, but she always found a way to find an excuse for his behavior.

Things felt different now with Kala in charge and we were all struggling with the adjustment I think. When Delgados was closed on Sunday evenings we had to walk to the Korean store on the Avenue if anything was needed in the house. It was on one of these treks that I almost got myself shot dead.

Early snow had been promised, but none arrived so she told me to bundle my "skinny little self" up and get on up to the store for some bread." I pouted, upset that I had to get off the phone (which was on for the moment). The wooden serving spoon came down on my knuckles so fast that I didn't even see it coming. I shook my hands back and forth trying to shake off the sting of wood and flesh meeting in pain.

"You sure are *smelling* yourself lately little girl," Kala said sarcastically, pulling a dollar out of her bra.

Smart enough to know that a reply wasn't necessary I pulled on my new purple wool coat. It was a gorgeous hand-me-down from the Goodwill that Kala said must have come from the Main Line. I slammed a hat on my head and grabbed the money from the kitchen table.

I was really mad at her for making me go alone, but Brother and Sonny (who still shared the same bed with Baby) had bad colds that she was trying to "clean up" before school in the morning. The word "pneumonia" still rumbled like tumbleweed in my brain. I slammed the screen door without a screen on my way out, and hurried away before she could come after me for doing it.

73

The fastest and safest way to get to the Korean store on the Avenue was to walk straight up 10th Street, past a line of 12 dilapidated row houses that had more broken windows than whole ones. Cornered by a Chinese restaurant and a greasy spoon, the block never lacked for traffic, but the reason I hated that walk most was because of Nubby.

It was Nubby, so nicknamed because of the two nubs that were his pinkie and ring fingers on his left hand. Some of the kids said he had eaten those fingers – that *his father had locked him, the runt of the family, deep in the bowels of their basement with no food or water for a year. He'd chewed on those two fingers to survive*. Another rumor was *that he blew them off in an explosion trying to break into the safe of the 'Watering Hole', the biggest bar in North Philly* after closing one Saturday night. But it was Nubby, not Mr. Nubby, Uncle Nubby or Cousin Nubby, just Nubby, 'cause it wasn't nobody who lived in the jungle or on the outskirts who thought Nubby was worth more than a nickname.

Nubby lived right in the middle of the block in a three -story house that more curved inward than stood straight. Three of the four front windows on the second and third floors were broken out. The windows on the first floor were boarded up. The last third floor window had some kind of white cotton sticking out of it that all the kids said was pair of his nasty drawers. In the summers, when the sidewalks were hot enough to fry an egg on them, Nubby would lie out across his marble steps with his hand in his pants just watching us as we tried to race past his house. I took to running as fast as I could down that block, both coming and going. But he always managed to say something before I got by him.

While scratching his crotch, he'd say stuff like, "You gettin' mighty thick," or "I got a piece of candy in here for you, girl."

Every girl I know hated to go that way and detested Nubby. Since he provided a service--corn liquor--to the neighborhood, the grown-ups just laughed at his comments and told us that he didn't mean no harm.

I was hoping against hope that the bitter weather would keep Nubby locked up somewhere in his house, maybe watching the Sunday football game or making another batch of his "death juice" as Kala called it. But there he was, hanging out his front door, his pregnant-looking yellow belly bursting from beneath a stained blue sweater. Flat bald head, and silver front tooth flashing in the grey of the day, he smiled as I approached. I was preparing myself to start running as soon as he started being nasty when something squishy and wet hit me on the back of my neck. Too shocked to move, I felt this thing slide, then land in the collar of my coat, warm, wet and hairy. A scream burst from my trembling lips and I reached for the offending object.

"I shot that one this morning," Nubby said with a laugh. "They tried to tell me I couldn't shoot 'em. Well you got the witness right there on your neck don't you girl."

It was a rat! A dead rat, big as a small cat, with its eyes popping out, hind legs shot to nothing but string, and blood dripping all over my hands.

"Nubby, why you do that to that girl?" a faraway female voice demanded. "You're just nasty."

75

"Mind your own business Edna. Girl is fine," he replied with a cackle. "Ain't you girl—fine that is? Been waiting an hour for one of y'all snot nose little heifers to wander your behinds (which he pronounced bee-hines) on by."

By this time, Nubby was in my face, his yellow teeth surrounding the one silver, gray smoke gushing from his mouth, and the smell of corn liquor overpowering everything. "Guess you'll stop talking about me now, won't you girl?"

The rat slipped from my hand and bounced off the cold sidewalk. His pink tongue was sticking out at me like a petulant little child's and his dead eyes stared at me with surprise. I wiped my hands on the front of my coat, leaving long read streaks on purple wool. Fear slipped out of my body like a deep breath.

"I'm gonna kill you for that!" I shrieked, getting up close, too close, to Nubby's ear as he bent over in laughter. "I'ma kill you *dead*."

As usual, Nubby was drunk so his reddened eyes watered with tears. Of course they weren't hurt tears, but the kind that come from a person laughing too hard at something.

Nubby raised his hand high above his head and slapped me so hard that spit flew right out of my mouth. I saw red, red and purple, as I rushed at him, scratching and kicking like some kind of wild thing. He knocked me to the ground, easily, like he was swatting a fat summer fly, but I was up again, raking his coatless back with my jagged fingernails. Nubby yelped, swung around and grabbed me by the back of my neck. Out of nowhere a gun appeared, pressing hard against the side of my head. I knew he was gonna kill me, saw the "I could care less" look in his bloodshot eyes. The cocking of the gun echoed throughout my brain and I closed my eyes not wanting Nubby's face to be the last thing I saw on this earth.

"Your momma stole my liquor," Nubby announced. "Guess this oughta' teach her a lesson."

The gunshot was as loud as I imagined one would be. Felt like I was hearing underwater. I held my breath waiting to see the clouds Kala had promised would be on one end, or the fire and brimstone on the other. There was no pain, no feeling of loss or warmth, only a cold breeze against my neck where Nubby's hand had rested a few seconds previously. I felt myself tilting backward, but braced my knees and came back up. "Well I'll be a monkey's uncle," I said aloud about walking into the after-life. Then I heard, "It's alright little girl. You can step away now."

My eyes more cracked than slid open and a white policeman's face, cool and stern, loomed huge above me. I followed his sea-blue eyes downward to where Nubby's head lay on the pavement, right next to the rat, his eyes now red from the blood running from the bullet hole in the side.

Somehow seeing him dead there felt worse to me than getting a bullet in my own head. Crazy as it might sound, I felt invaded by what the policeman had done. He wasn't from our neighborhood, our jungle, where we took care of our own business. I opened my mouth to scream but nothing came out. Blue, white and red flashed across my face and even though I know it shouldn't have been possible over the harsh whining of sirens, I swear I heard Kala's feet pounding as she ran down the street toward me. I knew the feel of her arms, felt the same as the night my daddy danced to death, warm, protective, safe. Then I gave into the blackness that was itching to slam my mind shut tight.

When I finally came back to my senses I was laying in our bed, undressed with a hot water bottle tucked beneath my back. It had gone cold, like the plate of food that sat on the table next to our bed. Kala's side was empty but I could hear soft strains of conversation floating from downstairs. Out of the frost-covered window I could see the stars twinkling like a light show. I thought of Nubby, that cold steel on the side of my head, and about how I hadn't run from death.

The next time we needed bread Kala sent Brother and Sonny. We'd lived too long with superstitions and she wasn't allowing another one to take hold. Brother was happy to report that there was big bloodstain on the ground in front of Nubby's house, a wide crimson circle with a dead rat somebody had kicked right to the middle of it. Sonny mentioned in passing that they'd seen our mother coming out of Nubby's front door with two men and a sheet full of something in her hand. He'd called out to her but she didn't seem to notice.

CHAPTER SEVEN – Miss Purina

After Nubby tried to kill me, folks in the concrete jungle started doing all kinds of nice stuff -

bringing a pie or a plate of cookies, pushing a quarter or dollar in my hand as I walked to school, or just asking, "How you doing today, child? You okay honey? That Nubby always been crazy." The people from the church came around a couple of times, once with a pot of chicken and dumplings that made me think that if they had that in heaven, I wouldn't mind dying so much. The second time they came they brought a roast chicken, macaroni and cheese and cabbage. Sonny and Baby ate so much of it that they both got sick to their stomachs and had to spend the night with a bucket at the bottom of their bed.

I started liking church a lot more after that. But the best gift we got over the next couple weeks came from Deacon Myles, who gave us a little black and white television from the church. It had more static than picture, but it was a television and we were happy to have it since the one we'd had disappeared with my mother months before.

It was Miss Patina (who we called Miss Purina behind her back) who brought up the subject of the empty room in our house. Funny how a person can forget something is there, even when they walk pass it every day. I only remembered her slightly, the boys not all, but Kala, she remembered her real well.

The evening Miss Patina showed up at our front door, Kala was locked in our bedroom studying for a math test she would take the next day. She'd stomped upstairs 30 minutes before mumbling something about how "a body couldn't even think around here." And she was right because our favorite television show, *The Jeffersons*, was on and we were in a full-blown argument over whether or not George should fire Florence for getting smart with him. Sonny and I thought he should, while Brother said absolutely not. Baby added his opinion by throwing his dirty socks at George, which made us burst into laughter again.

We were loud, so when Miss Patina knocked light and dainty on the door, we wouldn't have heard her if Baby didn't happen to lumber by the long window next to the front door and catch her shadow through the light green curtain.

"Somebody at door!" he yelled, giving us just enough information.

Brother, Sonny, and I, curled up nice and warm on the couch in bare feet, anticipating our next show, *Dallas*, did "rock, paper, scissors" to decide who would get up open the door. Sonny lost like he normally did because he was always picking paper. He stomped across the floor, face crushed up like he had bad gas pains or something, and snatched the door open wide. I wanted to slap him for not even asking who it was, but that meant losing my warm spot on the couch. Baby climbed up in my lap his fat legs spreading over mine like a blanket of skin. Felt delicious.

"Who are you?" Sonny barked at the visitor. A smile spread across my lips like melted butter 'cause I knew Kala would hear him from upstairs in a minute, come running, and twist his ear good for it.

"You Natty's boy?" the visitor responded.

"You got the wrong door, Miss," Sonny said softening his tone. "Ain't no Natty here."

"This is Natty's house. I knows it is 'cause I visited her here several times."

This lady had my attention now, so I pushed Baby roughly to the side. "Who is it Sonny?" I yelled, though I'd heard the whole conversation.

Curiosity overcame my need for warmth and I padded to the door in bare feet. She was a little thing. One of the tiniest women I'd ever seen and just her size caught my imagination. Worn lines ran through her face like trolley tracks and her hair was jet black, straight, and as long as her arm. A person meeting her on the street would have thought she was a white woman because her face lacked color, but it was her eyes that made me move to the side when she came stepping over the threshold. So black, they looked almost purple. Full of authority, those eyes said she wouldn't be taking no nonsense from nobody.

"Where Natty at?" the woman asked. "You girl, you over there, you her baby girl."

I hadn't heard Kala come down the stairs, but I turned now along with the boys as she pointed at Kala. "Where your grandmomma girl?"

"Miss Patina!" Kala exclaimed, a shocked look on her face. "I remember you. You were grandmomma's friend, the one who was nice to me." Then she surprised us all by pulling the tiny lady into a big hug. I don't think I'd ever seen Kala hug anybody who wasn't one of us. "They told me you were dead."

"Almost, not quite, could've been though." Miss Patina chuckled, handing me her long brown leather coat with the fur-lined collar. My fingers were itching to touch that fur, but I was afraid to mess it up.

"They tried to pronounce me dead, but I rose right back up again. I ain't had my mind for a while though. That's why it took me so long to come for Natty. Where she at girl? Where's my Natty?"

Kala rushed me into the kitchen to put on water for hot tea, but I nearly broke my neck trying to listen from in there. She settled Miss Patina on the couch and hollered at Brother to run and get a pillow to support her back. Baby, figuring that if she was allowed in the house she was okay, slid down the couch until his head met her shoulder. He kept grinning up at her like she was family.

"I remembered her," Miss Patina continued. "But I couldn't get away from them to come for her."

"Miss Patina, Grandmom Natty is gone. She's been gone for eight years at least." Kala paused, allowing her words to sink through. "Now where do you belong? I need to get you back home."

"Purina. Purina. Purina," Baby started chattering as I handed our guest a hot cup of tea in our best coffee mug.

"Cut it out Baby," Kala said, popping him soft like. "That's rude." Then she turned back to our company and explained, "He's a good boy, just acts up sometimes."

"I'm not blind, girl," Miss Patina replied. "I can see that boy ain't right, but he looks just like you, and like Natty, so that makes him alright with me. And there's no need to rush me out of here. They will come for me soon enough."

Miss Patina sipped on the cup of tea, took what I call a death breath, closed her eyes, and then leaned back on the pillow Brother had gotten off of my bed like she was suddenly too tired to go on.

"So they finally killed her didn't they?"

I was real confused by now. So was everybody else. We gathered around her, three of us sitting on the floor at her knees, two of us on either side of her on the couch. I looked up at her and saw that her face reflected a clarity and truthfulness that I have never seen on the face of an adult. Kala's eyes were filled with admiration and respect. Warmth flowed between them, making my heart flutter with jealousy. But then Miss Patrina began a story that made me forget all of that.

"Natty and I been friends since we were little girls down in Georgia. Her father worked the land of a man by the name of Bosley, and my daddy owned the farm that was attached to that land. We were only a year apart, so naturally we became the best of friends."

It was amazing to hear about my grandmomma, the woman who died before I really knew she was alive, before I had a chance to know her at all.

"After that piece of husband of hers died, Natty followed y'all momma up here. Felt bad about all that had happened to her. I followed Natty because there wasn't nothing left for me to hold on to down South. Both of our husbands were dead by then and we figured we weren't too old to start over," Miss Patina recalled with a smile. "Had big plans to get ourselves a house and sell fresh-baked rolls, to just live on. I know it sounds like a stupid dream, but we held on to that piece of dream until we couldn't no more."

"How come you let it go?" Brother interjected. My brothers, sister and I turned in unison and rolled our eyes at him.

"Leave that boy alone," said Miss Patina in Brother's defense. "He's handsome, like my husband."

We laughed at that, happy to break the tension in the room. Suddenly, I didn't want whoever was coming to take Miss Patina away, to come. It just looked to me that a lack of freedom would cripple a woman with her spirit.

"That dream just didn't work out boy," she continued. "We were used to disappointment and false hopes, your grandmomma wouldn't know life without 'em. Anyway, your momma, she'd was wronged, that's for sure. But it turned her mean and ugly, hateful towards your grandmomma, who couldn't stop him when he had his stupid mind made up about something.

It was Sonny's turn to interject. "What do you mean by that?" he asked.

"Well your grandmomma Natty, she moved up from Georgia when you were born," Miss Patina said, turning to Kala. "Not that she had much down there mind you, but she did have a little piece of house she lived in—and me. But I know she came because she was afraid for you, child."

Since we didn't know anything about our parents' pasts we were riveted to her story.

"But your momma hated her even more for coming. She wasn't here that long before she got real sick and your momma and daddy got worse. Left her in that room up there and—wait, which one of you sleeping in her room?" Miss Patina asked, sitting up a bit straighter. But then she broke into tears. "Oh, it don't matter much I guess. They were beating and starving her to death, and I promised her I would come get her out of here, but then I forgot and my son he never lets me out. Says I'm a danger to myself, but I remember Natty, yes I do."

"I remember her, too," Kala whispered so low you could hardly hear. She took care of me, gave me baths and played with me. I tried to get in that room but I was too little and when I cried for her they would beat me or put me to bed hungry. So I stopped looking or even thinking about her. Then one day they told me that she was dead and that door never was opened again."

I felt sorry for Miss Purina and Kala, for then and now. I had never known the ghost they spoke of so there was no pain in my heart as I listened.

Kala invited her to stay for dinner, and we were just settling into a meal of hamburgers and beans when Miss Purina's son came to collect her. He said he figured she'd head this way since she'd been talking about her friend Natty for days. I was sad to see her go, even after what she'd told us. Somehow just her talking about Grandmom Natty made me feel like I was wrapped up in her invisible bosom. It felt good to know that we did have someone who would have loved us if she'd had the chance. On her way out the door, Miss Patina told us something that would be very important, though we didn't know it at the time. But she insisted that her boy wait a minute and let her say her business.

"If you kids get into trouble, you call your Uncle Charlie, Charlie Nelson down Macon, Georgia," she said gripping Kala's young hands with her old. "You call him, you hear? Your momma's little brother, you call him."

Kala nodded looking as confused as the rest of us. Miss Purina never came back, and Kala said she might have been sent by grandmomma just to let us know she was okay. I never forgot her or what she said.

Three Fish

CHAPTER ONE - Blood

I could tell Kala was dreaming again. In her sleep she cried out and thrashed about wildly. My heart filled with anguish as I watched her face contort with pain. Her eyes opened to just the white part, un-seeing, I jumped from our bed although I was afraid the slightest movement would plunge her into a fantasy death. Miss Mickins told me once that when the "witch is riding someone's back" that it was dangerous to disturb them - that it could kill them. I was never sure what witch she was referring to, but in that moment, looking at my sister suffering, I felt she might be as close to death as I had been when Nubby put that gun to my head.

She woke up after a while, her hand reaching out for me and I climbed back beside her, buried my face in her back. Her breath was ragged which scared me further. Kala told me right after that dream that she didn't want me to know what it was about, but I told her I wouldn't be able to sleep until I knew. So she told me, and then I wished she hadn't.

She said, "I was swimming in the ocean again, but this time I was real happy, riding white capped waves and squeezing my toes against hard shells on the sandy bottom which should have been impossible since the water was so deep. Wasn't nobody but me in the whole big wide-open ocean and every time that cool water washed over my body I felt clean. I must've been in the water for hours 'cause before long I looked up and the sun was falling into the water in a beautiful orange and red ball.

"I knew right then that it was time."

"Time for what," I interrupted with my question.

"I didn't really know, just felt something was gonna happen that I would have no control over," she replied taking a real deep breath. "But when I turned to get out of the ocean I realized that I had gone so far that I could no longer see the shore. We was disconnected, me and the land, and I began to panic. Brown and green seaweed grabbed my arms, like those weeds that grow over on the empty lots and the harder I tried to get them off, the tighter they got.

"Don't think I want to hear no more Kala," I whispered, listening to a scurrying sound in between our silence. "There's a mouse in here."

"Well, I can't stop now. Once these dreams start pouring out I gotta finish. You're the only empty cup I got right now, so you gotta listen to the rest. Besides, that's the part when the fish came."

"What fish, the two fish with the big eyes?"

"No baby girl, these fish were small, real small, but they had a mouth full of vampire looking teeth."

"Like Blackular's?"

"Yeah, sort of like that. Was only three of 'em, but it felt like they were eating me from the inside out."

That's when I really, really, really began to regret asking about the dream.

"I was suspended in this kind of pain - not like when you fall and scrape your knee or even when your hand gets slammed in the door by mistake - this pain, it went straight into my soul. I closed my eyes and when I opened them again the ocean was full of blood and the waves, the waves they just got bigger and bigger until I thought for sure I was gonna' die from their force."

I wanted to close my eyes then, while she was talking, but I just knew if I did those waves would come for me too.

"Then one gigantic wave came over me, tossing and turning me like I was nothing, like a paper doll it could just bend and fold at its will. When it finished with me I was back on beach, alive, but I felt dead, like my spirit had been ripped right out of me."

By the time she finished that dream both of our faces were soaked with sweat and tears and I shivered next to her although it was warm in our room and didn't have a reason for it.

"You know girl, it ain't the good or the bad all the time. It's these little horrors in between that makes you just want to give up."

Those words scared me the most.

After that dream Kala just didn't seem to go back to acting normal. It was the way that she was acting different that I noticed more than the actual differences. She worked so hard to act like nothing was wrong that I knew it was. It was little things at first, like bursting into tears when Baby took a bite out of her straight A's report card. She sat in the middle of the floor and bawled until Baby climbed into her lap and began bawling too, and Sonny and Brother left their game of checkers upstairs to see what was happening. They ran to hug her 'cause they thought "the people" was finally coming to take us away.

Or how she tried to take my head off for being five minutes late back from the store where she had sent me to get a loaf of bread. Bobby Taylor had asked to carry the bag, though it was light as a feather, so I had walked a little bit slower than normal. She met us at the door with one of my father's thick, leather belts, had it raised high above her head to hit me, but dropped it suddenly just to walk away without another word. Bobby Taylor never did carry my bread bag again. We spent a month like this, with her hiding her sun behind a sky full of rain. Things came to a head, like things do, gushing out just like pimple insides— surprising you and leaving a sore spot 'cause you've been picking at it for a while. But what surprised me most was that it was Sonny who was the one who took the top off the blackhead.

Thanksgiving had come and gone the week before. We'd celebrated with a church basket stuffed with a turkey almost bigger than our small stove, candied sweet potatoes, green beans, and two fresh-baked apple pies from the sisters in the white hats that left our fingers sticky and our bellies aching.

The day was disappearing in a glare of glorious orange and I was helping Baby with his pretend homework, 'cause Kala insisted that he get some learning too. Kala was making mayonnaise and government cheese sandwiches to go along with canned chicken soup. We heard Brother screaming from across the street, five houses down and I swear my blood turned cold from the sound of it. He reached the door just as Kala pulled it wide.

"The man got Sonny!"

He let go of his two-sizes-too-large pants, a gift from the Salvation Army, and they dropped to his ankles revealing brown and gray on the spots where he hadn't used the Vaseline that morning. The look of fear in his eyes stopped a laugh from escaping my throat.

"They got Sonny I tell you!"

"Who has him?" Kala demanded to know, mayonnaise jar and butter knife shaking like a rattle in her hands.

"The Delgados said he was stealing, but he wasn't. I swear it."

Now I knew, and she did too, that it was Brother who was stealing 'cause Sonny would rather hold his hand over a hot stove than take something that didn't belong to him. But she didn't take the time to argue that point just then. Instead she stomped right out of the front door, slamming the screen door with the missing screen so hard that if it had a screen it would have popped out. She headed toward Delgado's, mayonnaise jar swinging in front of her. I marched beside her, dragging a smiling Baby behind me.

Outside, the crowd that had gathered around the small corner store parted when we arrived, licking their lips in preparation for what they knew was coming. And I hate to say they got it, not because we were ever ashamed of protecting each other, but rather because they are bloodsucking vultures that looked at us as another meal to satisfy their lust for evil doings. (Sometimes I run off on these tangents. But I started this story, so I gotta finish it "because it just ain't right to leave a girl hanging off a ledge when you got the rope to save her," is what Kala would say about leaving a story without an ending.)

Kala was never one for words with anybody but me. She paused only long enough to see that Sonny was being held on the ground by the Delgado boys, snot running out of both nostrils and the side of his face swelling to the size of a peach.

When she saw that he wasn't dead, she swung that mayonnaise jar with a pitcher's arm and busted the oldest one right atop his wavy black head. Blood ran down the back of his left ear, and he got to screaming and hollering. People started pointing and laughing, which made Baby start laughing too. The Delgado boy had to release Sonny 'cause he couldn't hold him and his bloody head too. Then the other brother dropped Sonny's arm and went for Kala, charging at her with his shoulders, steam rolling her onto the hard concrete. Before we knew it, fists were flying as fast as the cuss words from our mouths as we attacked and were attacked.

Mrs. Delgado hollered "I gonna call the policia!" from the second floor window and Mr. Delgado, looking forlorn and weary, rushed out the pull his son off of Kala. They exchanged a telling look as he hustled his two sons back into the store and waved the crowd away with one of his fat arms.

94

Later, over bowls of hot chicken soup and thick government cheese sandwiches minus the mayonnaise, we declared it a draw. But I knew for sure that the Delgados weren't ever going to mess with Sonny again. I could tell Kala was worried about our weekly delivery from Mr. Delgado, but as usual, it magically appeared the next week.

Brother, who was very proud of his role in saving his brother and still pretending that he wasn't the one who started the whole mess, was totally shocked when Kala sent him to bed early with no food or cartoons. I washed the dishes as she tucked in Sonny and Baby, sneaking Brother a sandwich when she thought I wasn't looking. When she left for work, she looked wore out to me, but she refused to stay home.

We agreed later that it must have been the #23 trolley car running right in front of our house that woke me 'cause I normally sleep like a rock. Immediately I noticed that our bed was cold and then I felt the wetness. According to the calendar, winter was scheduled to begin in two weeks but bitter winds had blown in from some region where they were welcome in early December.

Half-drunk with sleep, the other half with curiosity, I stumbled to the bathroom and tripped over her big feet that were sticking out of a crack in the door. I would have screamed if she hadn't pressed her forefinger to her lips real quick to keep me from doing so. "It was a baby," she said, sad like. "It was his baby."

95

I'm not the fastest cowgirl at the rodeo, but I had already figured that one out. I'm embarrassed to say that at her words, my bladder burst and lukewarm pee squeezed between my crossed legs and collected at my ankles.

"You know I gotta pee soon as I wake up," I said accusingly.

"I know," she replied. "But I'm too tired to move right now. Help me up."

Now you need to understand, I love this girl more than I love myself sometimes, but at that moment, her blood and fluids soaking the bathroom floor, a bloody looking lump of thing in her arms, I turned and ran back to our room and slammed the door shut, hard. Sitting on the edge of our bed, tears streaming down my ashen face, I recalled her fish dream.

Even though we didn't talk about it right away that don't mean I don't know what happened, didn't listen, with pee burning my butt, to her crying for about an hour before I finally heard her footsteps moving slowly down the steps. When the house is quiet, only filled with the soft snores of Baby and Brother, you can bout hear everything, so it wasn't hard to hear the backdoor open and close with a hard click.

I tiptoed down the stairs and peered out one of the double kitchen windows. Watched her for another hour, guilt backing up my throat so thick I could hardly breathe, as she dug a tiny grave with her bare hands, and put the bloody bundle there. She patted the dirt with two hands over and over, like she was trying the burp that dead baby in the grave. It broke me, seeing her like that - broke her too, for a while.

CHAPTER TWO - Broken

For the first time in my short life, the day after she buried that baby and poured Clorox all over the tiny grave to keep away the strays, Kala didn't get out of bed. The house felt different. I lay there a moment trying to identify the feeling, and then I knew. A strange warmth flowed from her side of the bed - didn't feel like morning. She was balled up, her long legs wrapped around the quilt we'd shared for as long as I could remember.

I thought, *she must be dead*. Although I was afraid to do so, I was more afraid not to, so I laid my head against her back to see if she was breathing. She was, her heart skipping every other beat like a rusty bicycle wheel, spoke broken, but still useable. Silently, I wiped the tears from my eyes with the back of my hand and went downstairs to get Sunday breakfast, which consisted of a bowl of cold cereal and half an orange apiece.

I sent up a bowl by the repentant Brother, but she refused to eat. The cup of chocolate milk I sent an hour later also came right back, still full to the rim. I was worried but wouldn't let on to the little ones. Even Baby understood something was wrong and spent the day playing quietly. Sonny attempted to read her a few chapters of his latest reading assignment and received a cold stare for his trouble. She lay frozen inside, and nothing we said or did was enough to thaw her. Baby, finally taking Sonny's cue, climbed in the bed beside her and fell asleep.

The next day she didn't get up or go to school. Now I was *really* worried since I couldn't remember a day she'd missed school or allowed us to miss. She insisted that I get the boys ready and then leave myself. I dropped Baby off at the daycare center three blocks up even though it was on the way to her school and six blocks from mine. For the first time in their lives, Brother and Sonny had to walk to school by themselves and I truly understood how alone she must feel taking care of us every day. On my way to my school, I fought back the tears gathering in my eyes because I was afraid that if I let them start, they would never stop.

The math teacher gave a surprise quiz. I gave him a zero. In my reading class I stumbled over words that were below my level and drew such a scary picture in my art class that Mrs. Lucas the young art/music teacher sent me to the principal "just to have a talk." Kala would be gone when I returned home, I was sure of it.

It started raining right after I picked up Baby and I had to carry him and my book bag, so I was exhausted by the time we got home. We entered by the backdoor because I just didn't want to come in the way she may have left. But there she was, blue scarf wound around her head, flipping pancakes in the air. I couldn't speak. I could only stand there and let the smell of the cooking batter enter my nose.

"Standing in that door like that you gonna' get a death of a cold," Kala said without turning around. "But if you do you still going to school in the morning." Baby slid off my back and ran over to grab her legs. My heart swelled with so much love for her that I thought I would smother inside out. "Brother and Sonny will be down in a minute for dinner. Set the table."

It wasn't but a week after that Kala and my mother came to blows. Not how you might be thinking, not with fists like with the Delgados, but war all the same 'cause my mother showed up as usual with a bag full of hurt and pain.

Because it was the weekend and the rule was homework got done on Sunday afternoons, we were all gathered around the small black and white television. It was Baby's turn to hold the coat hanger up so we could see without all the white snow. Kala was sitting on the couch braiding Brother's hair. He had decided he wanted it to grow instead of taking the chance on Mr. Turner cutting it again. I didn't blame him since last time blood was running down the side of his face when the old barber was done.

"Oh, that's just sweat," was Mr. Turner's answer when Brother had questioned the dribble. But a big patch was missing out of the boy's head and he did have an unexplained sore the next day.

Sonny and I had seats on the floor on either side of Brother and we took turns tickling Kala's ankles, which made her pop us with the comb every time she finished a braid. Our heads turned in unison to the sound of the turning doorknob. I remembered suddenly that I had run next door to borrow some Dixie Peach from Miss Mickins and had forgotten to lock the door when I got back.

My mother more stumbled than walked in and Kala gave me a dirty look. We all pretended like we didn't see her. Brother's arm hardened like a brick and Sonny scurried from the floor to join Kala on the couch. Baby continued to bend over to watch *Speed Racer*, his favorite cartoon.

"Well, ain't this nice?" my mother jeered.

And with those words I knew it would be trouble. See, we lived by signals, measured our sense of safety by how high she was when she came home. If she came in without speaking and went straight to the bathroom located in the hallway between the living room and kitchen, then she was already heavily drugged and wouldn't be much trouble. Mid-high brought with it manageability filled with phony hugs and kisses as her eyes roamed about the room looking for anything of value. But if she were near sober, like she was now with her sarcastic tongue and cold, vicious eyes, it would be a miserable time filled with ugly words, threats and tears.

"Well, ain't *this* nice," she repeated as we stared at her warily. Baby, finally realizing the change of mood, unceremoniously dropped the hanger and static filled the room.

"All my children gathered here waiting for me. Just like Erica Kane and 'em on the soap opera." She laughed at her private joke but we just stared.

Kala rolled her eyes and pushed Sonny off the sofa. "Go get the hanger boy." I felt sorry for Sonny then 'cause he looked like he was going to be sick right there on the spot. But he rushed over to the television to grab the hanger. Baby took his place on the couch laying his round head in Kala's lap.

"Think I'll join y'all," my mother said, taking a seat on the couch. "How you doing, honey? Everything okay with you?"

I couldn't look at her. I kept my head down and continued digging at a hole in my jeans until Kala slapped my hand.

"Stop that," she commanded. "You need those jeans."

"You don't have to slap the girl. She ain't your child," my mother said. I could feel the heat rising between them and I wanted to move real bad, but I was afraid if I did, the couch would burst into flames and kill us all.

Kala turned to me then, her eyes kinda' dead-like. "Take the boys and go outside," she said. When I didn't move 'cause I was frozen in between their inferno, she said, "Go on. It's gonna' be okay."

Since I trusted her with my life, our lives, I handed the boys their coats and put on mine. I grabbed Baby by the hand and went out the door followed slowly by Brother and Sonny. Sonny pulled the door closed but the windows were up 'cause project housing always have at least one room that's always burning up no matter the season - ours was our living room. Through that open window, sitting on a cold step that made my butt feel like the floor of an ice rink, we listened.

"You need to go. There's nothing here for you anymore," Kala yelled at my mother.

"Who the hell are you?" my mother screamed. "I'm your mother." I knew that it hurt Kala real bad to hear those words.

"You haven't been a mother for a real long time," my sister shot back.

"What? What you think, I'm not good enough?"

I could tell by the sound of her voice that she was enraged and needing a shot of whatever it was she shot in her arm. Noodle, Mrs. Mickins's oldest son, the one who robbed a bank and was hiding from the police, came out on the adjoining cement porch. Should have been minding his own business but he stood there like he couldn't hear the shouting, but I knew he did.

"We don't have nothing, you've stolen it all," Kala hissed. "You're a thief and a liar. No good, no good."

Her voice was strained, like she was someone on the verge of tears who was refusing to let them fall. Baby wrapped his chubby little arms around my neck and Sonny covered his ears, but Brother stomped off the porch and headed down the street although he knew he would get in trouble for doing it. I didn't bother to call him back because, truthfully, I wanted to run away, too.

"I'm not letting you take their television," Kala declared. "That's all they got."

So that was it. My mother wanted the little old raggedy thing that the church had given us. "Let her have it," I said softly. "Just let her have it."

My mother unveiled more of her addict logic: "You owe me," she said. "I know you took that money the night your father died. I know he had money in his pocket."

"Owe you? Oh my God, you're crazy," Kala said incredulously.

"You robbed your own father while he was lying on the floor dying. You robbed him didn't you? Didn't you?"

I wanted to vomit, the memory of his death coming back full force. Instead, I put an arm around Sonny who was rocking back and forth. Baby looked up at me with sad brown eyes and it was then I realized that this was the only time he stopped smiling, when my mother came around.

"He robbed *me*!" Kala screamed. "He stole the only thing I had, the only thing that belonged to me, and you let him. You let him! You knew and you let him!"

"Didn't hurt you none, now did it?" my mother said with a chuckle. I thought of her as a witch at that second. "Look at you. You look good girl. He made you a woman."

After that, the voices stopped. Noodle, without an excuse to be standing there listening, opened their screen door and went back inside his house. With my knees wobbling and my head throbbing, I handed a solemn Baby to Sonny and tiptoed back inside. There was my mother struggling with the television cord, trying to get it out of the socket. Kala was staring at her with murder in her eyes. It was the same look she had that night when she was cooking the grits. I was extremely relieved that there were no pots on the stove at that moment.

Then she moved, actually looked like she flew, across the room to where my mother had finally gotten the plug out and was bending to pick up our pitiful little black and white set. Kala grabbed her by her nappy hair with more strength and power than a girl her age should have in her body and dragged her straight through to the kitchen, stopping only when they reached one of windows.

"Look out there!" Kala yelled. I could tell my mother was stunned, but it was wearing off fast. She swung her skeleton arms back and forth trying to get free.

"I said look! See that there? See that spot all white from bleach? That's where his daughter is buried!" Kala was crying now, snot and tears running free.

For a second—and it happened so fast that I wasn't sure that I could trust my eyes—I saw hurt, regret, and maybe even sorrow in my mother's permanently yellowed eyes. But then she opened her mouth.

"So?" she taunted. "I had five kids by him."

104

Not another minute. Not another minute could I let her talk like that. Before I knew it, I had that piece of television in my arms, thrusting it at her, and pushing her out the back door.

"Thank you!" she called back, walking right by the mound Kala had directed her to, gripping the television tightly.

This is the only time that I can remember Kala letting me be the big sister, even if it was just for a little while. "I hope she dies," someone declared. Wasn't until later that night that I realized that *I* had said those words.

CHAPTER THREE – Fire Starter

Another one of those little horrors Kala saw coming in her fish dream involved Brother. We were all hurt, angry little children, but Brother's anger seemed to go deeper than ours. Since my parents weren't around to catch it, he took his anger out on us every chance he got. Things got really bad about two weeks after my mother's last visit. With no television to entertain us in the evenings, we spent a lot of time playing checkers, card games and reading books. An early December cold snap covered the city and froze our little house along with the rest of the city. Trying to make some extra money for Christmas, Kala went to work earlier than usual. She made us peanut butter and marshmallow sandwiches (my favorite), and left me in charge of the boys. She wasn't gone an hour before I noticed that Brother was missing.

"I dunno know," Sonny mumbled when I asked him about Brother's whereabouts. My suspicious gaze didn't make him change his mind so I turned to Baby who was sitting quietly and staring at a book. I knew he wouldn't have an answer but I asked him anyway.

An hour later, I was beyond frantic. With 75 identical houses surrounding twin high-rise buildings, I had no idea where to start looking for Brother. We had very few friends because Kala didn't give us a wide berth like most of the concrete jungle kids had. Brother was too young to be in pool hall where the teenage boys liked to hang out, and for sure he wasn't at the church for bible study. As the night went on, I wore dents into kneecaps praying that God would send Brother home. Still, I took care of the boys like I knew Kala would want me to. I put Baby to bed and ordered Sonny to clean out the tub and take his bath. I tried to do homework to distract myself from a thousand blood-curdling thoughts building in the back of my mind.

I drifted in and out of sleep keeping watch at the front window for Brother's red zip-up jacket and navy blue cap. (I chose to wait by the front door because it was less scary than the back). At 11:00 P.M. I was startled by the creaking of the screen door with the missing screen. Then someone banged on the front door. I rushed to open it, and seeing that it was Brother, I couldn't decide whether I was going to pull him into a big hug or slap him silly for running off. I hugged him.

It took a moment for me to notice that something about him, besides being out so late, wasn't right. I

106

took in the black smudge on Brother's face along with the self-satisfied glow he seemed to have. And then I smelled it - gasoline. Brother smelled like he had taken a bath in it.

"What did you do Brother?" I whispered as he pulled away from my grip. "I'm gonna tell!"

But he just smiled, like he does when you threaten him 'cause no punishment has ever been big enough.

"Kala will be home any minute. Get a bath and get in bed before she gets here," I ordered. In that moment I made up my mind that I didn't want to know any more and didn't want Kala to know either.

Seven-thirty the next morning, after Kala hummed "Sweet Hour of Prayer", we finished blessing our hot bowls of oatmeal, and she slapped Sonny's hand for trying to steal her piece of half-burnt toast, the police knocked on the door. The knock was for show 'cause they were through the front and back doors before we could answer either, guns drawn, badges out.

"There's been a fire in Building One, eighth floor. The person who started it lives here," one of the cops barked. "Hundreds could have been killed."

Kala was shocked; I could see that in the way her eyebrows crawled upward with each word. Meanwhile, Baby smiled and pointed. "Policeman! Policeman!" I looked over at Brother, who was peering down at his bowl of oatmeal. Sonny, breakfast forgotten, stood trembling in the nearest corner.

Finally, raising her glass casually, Kala took a gulp of milk and found her voice. "Ain't nobody here that did that sir, only kids live here."

My hands began to flutter. I feared that they would learn the truth. A bit of oatmeal flew off my spoon and hit one of the officers right on his big red cheek. "Sorry," I squeaked, refusing to let the steel in his prying eyes dig into my head where thoughts of Brother's gasoline-smelling clothes were floating around.

"We got witnesses says the arsonist lives here."

"They're wrong," Kala insisted.

Brother kept right on eating like the cops wasn't even there. I looked down at his feet and saw he had on his winter boots instead of the gasoline-scented Converse sneakers he had on the night before. I would have crossed myself like the sisters over at the convent did if I was Catholic, but instead I said a silent prayer of thanksgiving and held my breath.

"We have a search warrant."

"Search then, ain't nothing here," Kala said.

I felt like I was going to pee my pants right then and there. They were going to find Brother's clothes and arrest him! Kala would probably kill me for not watching him, for allowing him to get outside. I wanted to lay my face right down in that oatmeal and die, but she pinched my upper arm and gave me a look that said, "*Hold your head up girl*".

"We gotta get to school so make it quick," she told the police while guiding Sonny back into his chair. "We had a death recently. The kids are still upset."

Fifteen minutes later they came down empty handed, blank looks on their faces—the kind you only get from being wrong about something that should have been right. They left as fast as they had come.

Leaving our breakfast bowls on the table (something we never did because of rodents), Kala rushed us out to school. I spent the entire day trying to figure out why the police didn't find Brother's clothes smelling of gasoline and trouble. Three o'clock came quicker than I'd hoped and I walked home making Brother hold my hand, which made the other kids laugh at him. I didn't care. He wasn't getting away from me again.

When we got home, she was waiting. "Sit down," she said just to me, waving Brother and Sonny upstairs and commanding them to take Baby with them. "Oh, and Sonny you call me the minute Brother tries to sneak out of y'all room and listen at the stairs." Brother gave her a surprised look, but didn't say anything. He followed Sonny and Baby up the wooden steps. I never noticed before how hollow those stairs sounded before that moment.

Kala sat me next to her on that ratty old "found" couch and told me why the police didn't find Brother's gasoline-smelling clothes. See, when she'd returned to the concrete jungle, at about 1:00 A.M. like she normally does, she and Esther from around the corner and four houses down saw the smoke pouring out of

Building One even before they got off the bus. Five or six fire trucks were lined up and firemen were running from one place to another trying to figure out how to get their ladders up to the eighth floor. People, hundreds of them, were standing around the front of the building in their bathrobes and pajamas.

Somebody mentioned that a fire had started right in front of Billy Kettles apartment. There was gasoline all up and down the fire escape. Mothers were crying and upset. The men were talking about how they were going to find the S.O.B. and give him a Viking burial. I wasn't sure what that was but thought it wise not to interrupt Kala just then.

After only a few minutes of listening to the gossip and knowing that she didn't have the power to help anyone, she hurried home 'cause she was worried. Noodle from next door was waiting for her on the stoop.

"See that fire over there?" he asked her, swaying from the forty bottle of Colt 45 he held in his hand.

"Got to be blind not to," she'd answered him opening the screen door with the missing screen.

"Check your boys," he warned. "One of them ain't right."

She turned around, looked him dead in the eye, and recalled the fish dream she'd had about all "the little terrors." Heart pounding, Kala leaped up the stairs and stopped short in front of the boys' bedroom door. Sonny, Brother, Baby—she counted them slow like the number three was too high for her to comprehend. Then she smelled the gasoline. Saw that Brother's clothes, in a pile on his side of the bed, were saturated.

"If I had flicked a match to check them, we'd all gone up in flames," she recalled.

Kala said she went outside holding Brother's clothes in her arms. There were burnt pieces of clothing, furniture and paper floating about in the deep black night. "I stood on the front stoop just like the statue of bronze Harriet in the center of my school, frozen but determined to do something."

Police cars zoomed pass, lights flashing red and blue, but the men inside didn't look her way. Out of a dark corner Noodle emerged. She wondered how nobody ever saw him, as light as he was, until he was right up on them.

"The #23 is coming," he said, taking the pile from her arms. He put them in a brown paper bag and sprinkled vinegar all over it. "I feel like taking a ride tonight. If a girl I know was smart, she'd do a little cleaning tonight with a lot of bleach while her kids are asleep."

With that, Noodle walked off the porch with the only evidence that Brother had started that fire. Kala told me she still don't know why he did it, but when he took the long seat in the back of the trolley she lifted her arm and waved like a girl welcoming home her soldier. (I smiled at that; I couldn't even imagine Kala doing that). Then I got a hive of bees in my stomach watching the way her eyes lit up a bit and she chewed on her bottom lip as she talked about what Noodle had done.

"The way I see it, Brother must have eavesdropped when I told you about my search for your mother while Baby was sick—how I found her, and what she was doing at the time. So that hole, which started as a small pebble of hurt, has grown into a big empty well. He is determined to drown himself in his own anger," Kala said slowly.

"Brother has a hole in his heart where a mother or father should be," she said gently, lifting my face between her hands so that our noses touched lightly. "We all have our holes, but carrying so much hurt and pain inside of that skinny little body just gets too heavy some time and he got to let it out." She took a deep breath and reflected on the people who were put out of their little piece of the jungle because of that fire. How he could have killed those people because of that sadness inside him. "We have to watch out for Brother until that hole in his heart repairs itself," she concluded.

Tears filled my eyes as I wondered if there was anything in this world that could fill such a big hole, but I nodded my head in agreement anyway.

CHAPTER FOUR: Noodle Heaven

Two evenings later, as I was sweeping the living room floor and watching Brother out of the corner of my eye, there was soft knock on the door. He moved to answer it but I yelled, "I'll get it!"

It was Noodle (actually, his full nickname is Spaghetti Noodle 'cause he is so tall and light.) There he was grinning at me from the other side of the screen door with the missing screen.

"What you want?" I demanded with my hands on my hips, 'cause I didn't really like Noodle or trust him, even if he did save Brother. He laughed at me then, long and hard, and I gripped that broom handle so hard that one of my knuckles cracked. Wanted to crack him upside the head is what I wanted. I said "What you want, Noodle!"

"Leave him alone," said Brother who had joined me at the door. They shared a secret look. I was fuming.

"What's the matter Sister Girl?" Noodle teased, suddenly looking so handsome that it made my teeth hurt. "Am I disturbing your sweeping?"

Lord help me, I blushed.

"What time is the bus Noodle?"

It was Kala, who had swept into the room so silently that it seems like she'd flown. She had red lipstick on her lips, looking a mess. Her cleaning uniform was starched and ironed like I'd never seen before.

"Fifteen minutes, about," he responded, stepping through the door and forcing me to step back or be knocked over. Noodle was in our house! I was shocked by the sparks shooting between them. One trolley ride with some gasoline-soaked clothes had led to this? I was furious! Even worse, Kala started giving

113

me instructions in front of him, like I didn't know them all by now. Brother was looking up to him like he was "somebody," and Sonny, the traitor, shook his hand. Baby had to have a handshake too, and Noodle lifted him easily into the air and twirled him around until he begged to be let down. And the whole time Kala was standing there just watching with this silly look that I wanted to slap off her face.

"Why you worried about the bus Noodle?" I asked since everybody seemed like they'd lost their minds. "She's going to work. She don't have no time for you."

Kala gave me a cold look that said "*SHUT UP!*"

"Esther ain't going to work tonight. So Noodle's gonna ride downtown with me, make sure I'm safe."

"Yeah, to make sure she's safe," he echoed with what I took as a sly look about him.

After that night Noodle was around all the time. He started coming over for dinner, then riding with her to work every night and riding back most. He took Sonny, Brother and even Baby out in the back parking lot in the evenings to play stickball before dinner and helped them with homework while she got dressed for work. Truthfully, I never did like Noodle, but everybody else seemed to so I tolerated his presence.

One night, after he'd ridden the trolley with her to work and come back, Noodle was standing on the front stoop smoking a cigarette 'cause Miss Mickins wasn't allowing that in her house. I pulled on my coat and came out to talk to him.

"Why you hanging around here Noodle?" I asked in the most pleasant voice I could muster.

He laughed, like he always did when I spoke to him. "Cause I like y'all, Sister Girl. Don't you know that by now?"

"We've had a lot of hurt and we don't need no more," I retorted.

He looked at me kinda' shocked, like I shouldn't be so wise for my age or something like that.

"See those buildings down there?" he asked, pointing south toward downtown where the top of the gigantic skyscrapers were lit up like a carnival of white. "One day I'm going to be down there, Sister Girl, 'cause ain't no hurt at the top of them buildings."

It was my turn to look at him funny like. I was wondering if he'd been smoking some "red or gold" and hallucinating as a result.

"Y'all going in that direction, too."

"What you talking about Noodle?" I asked.

"See, Sister Girl," he started stepping down from the stoop, raising his arms towards the stars and closing his eyes. "See this great big monstrosity, it was built to hold us in, make us feel like it's impossible to escape its concrete walls, boxed-in dreams. But some of us see pass the end of the trolley line, see pass those tall buildings where we work at night cleaning toilets and emptying other people's thoughts and determination from the waste cans. Some of us see 'one day,' and we reach for

115

something that hasn't been promised or even allowed. But we see it anyway, beyond this red, green-less place." His eyes filled with tears as he looked at me. "Some of us just see out."

I wanted to hug him tight for his dreaming ways, but instead I turned toward the lights of the tall buildings of Center City Philadelphia, pulled my coat closer, and asked, "Why'd you rob that bank Noodle?"

"Why didn't you?" he asked, shaking his head as he walked into his house, leaving me alone to wonder about that.

I found a place in my heart for Noodle. Kala was happy and relieved, but I think more relieved since we were so close. We all fell into a comfortable routine that was interrupted less and less often by my mother. It was official that Kala and Noodle were "going together" and the gossips started gossiping even though the cold weather kept most folks locked away in their little piece of government heaven.

"Everybody got that somebody that's got to be in everybody else's business," is all Kala said when I told her about the rumor that she Noodle were sleeping together.

Our "somebody" was Mrs. Daisy Smithfield, seven doors down on the same side of the street. I'm sure I'd never seen beyond the head, neck and arms of Mrs. Smithfield and I didn't think anybody else had either, although Sassy Mickins, Noodle's younger sister swore she'd seen her out at the meat market buying a whole pig just last week. Sassy always was a liar, but nobody called her one to her face 'cause it wasn't worth the hurt feelings to be right.

But we had all grown up around the sound of Mrs. Smithfield's voice calling out to the community since she was one of the first residents to move in when the place was built 17 years ago. It was always, "Hey Mr. Turner, business kind of slow today ain't it?" and "Hey boy, you in the red shirt over there, come run to the store for me. I need a Stanback and three dollars' worth of cheese!" she would yell throwing a couple of dollars out the window. "You can keep the change."

There were all kinds of stories about why Mrs. Smithfield never left that window. *She didn't have any legs. She was hiding from the police. She was waiting for the missing Mr. Smithfield to walk by one day and say hello.* There were all kinds of stories, but we took turns standing under that window sometimes to go to the store for her, to get that change which was only a quarter or dime but enough to get a treat that we wouldn't have otherwise. She was as much a part of the concrete jungle as the numerous cracks in the sidewalk or the group of teenage boys throwing dice on the corner for empties that could be redeemed for a nickel apiece.

The cold had forced the closing of windows and fast-paced walking to the store when necessary, but Mrs. Smithfield stayed at her post, her bedroom window on the second floor at the front of her house. With a pillow resting like a shield against the frozen windowsill, she took her position every morning at about 10:00 and remained on duty until at least an hour after dark, rain or shine. So it was only natural that when Noodle and Kala had their first kiss on the

117

corner of 10th and York as they waited for the #23 trolley she would be a witness to the event.

"Y'all kids need to stop that nastiness!" she called down to them, secretly happy, I believe to finally have some new gossip to share.

Noodle couldn't stand Mrs. Smithfield or her son Frankie who everyone suspected of being the one in the Freddy Kruger mask who snatched our Halloween treat bags. (Rumor was he fed candy corn one at a time to his mother, like grapes.) According to Kala, Noodle retorted, "Mind your own douche bag business!"

So Mrs. Smithfield started screaming for Frankie, who ran to the window to see who had upset his momma.

Noodle added, "Tell your fat momma if she got out of that window sometimes and took a walk she might lose a pound or two in something besides those rolls of belly fat!" He was laughing, but Kala pulled at his arm gently to try to stop what she knew would be coming if she didn't defuse the situation at that moment. But Noodle, who was irritated that Mrs. Smithfield had interrupted a moment that it had taken him months to build up to, would not be silenced.

"Don't say nothin' else about my momma unless you want a foot up your butt," Frankie threatened. (OK, he said the other word but I don't feel that's necessary to repeat to explain the situation.)

And much as I hate to admit it, Noodle knew that you can't talk about a person's momma without it being a challenge. And Frankie, who'd had a crush on

Kala for as long as I can remember, couldn't let himself be put down in front of his momma. He disappeared from the window and appeared outside in about 30 seconds flat. Since the windows had been shut tight due to the cold, and most of the televisions were tuned to the latest sitcom or the 76ers game, it took a minute or two for the residents of the jungle to notice that something major was about to go down. Our house was only three doors from the trolley stop, and Sonny, who spent a lot of time just looking out, saw them first.

Frankie Smithfield, with an old mop handle that we borrowed sometimes to play stickball, approached with all the rights and lack of reservation that belonged to the offended. Noodle stood there, his arms folded across his chest like he wasn't worried at all. Kala screamed for them to stop. The #23 trolley came at exactly 7:00 PM, and then the driver sped away barely hitting the brake. A crowd was gathering on the street and in the windows. A light snow began to fall as I rushed out to the corner, Brother on my heels. Sonny, with Baby at his feet, kept his position in the living room window.

"Take it back about my momma or I'll kill you!" Frankie screamed.

It was an empty threat; no one expected someone to die on that corner. But the tension shot up like a space shuttle into the atmosphere.

"What part you want me to take back Frankie - the part about your momma needing to mind her business, or the part about her being an old douche bag?"

"Frankie! Frankeeee boy get on in here!" Mrs. Smithfield called from her window. "Don't get into a fight with that trash."

All the Mickins's, who had appeared as quickly as you turning around three times, stared up at her window. Miss Mickins, one of the sweetest, kindest people you could know, rolled her eyes and mumbled something about "God having mercy on fools and fat people."

"Your momma's calling you Frankie boy," Noodle teased. I wished with all my heart that he would just shut up and let this thing die. Kala wished it too. I could tell by the way she kept tugging at Noodle's coat sleeve and telling him to "come on in the house." I think Frankie wanted to back off, I really do, but Noodle had pushed him in a corner and if he didn't stand up and do something about it now even the little kids would be trying to push him around.

A couple things happened all at the same time, so I'm just a little unclear today about what really took place. But what I remember was that Frankie, who was dark skinned although his momma was reddish-brown, lifted that mop handle to swing at Noodle, who just happened to taking a congratulations from one of his brothers on winning the verbal battle. Frankie swung it with all his might just as Kala was moving in front of Noodle to take his arms and pull him away. When that broom handle came down across her back, it cut through the thickness of her navy blue Goodwill wool pea coat and knocked her to her knees. The silence that followed bounced off of the cement, plaster and glass of the projects, travelled up and down the indoor fire escapes of Building One and Building Two, raced out of the chimneys on top of them, and shot toward the coal-colored sky. I begin to pray in earnest for Frankie Smithfield. Miss Mickins, who was standing with Noodle and her five other kids, opened her mouth to say something to Sassy but suddenly turned crimson, her lips half open, tongue frozen mid-sentence. She fell to the ground dead as a doornail.

The crowd dispersed immediately, like roaches, running wildly toward safety as Brother and I ran over to help Kala up from the ground. Noodle and his brother and sisters were stunned of course. Sassy was turning 'round and 'round like my mother did the night of the hot grits, crying "No momma, no!"

It was a ghastly circus as police and emergency response came 20 minutes too late to do anything but collect poor Miss Mickins from the cold cement and cart her off to the morgue. The other kids followed, but Noodle was dragged forcibly into our house by Kala and two of his friends since he was still wanted for bank robbery.

CHAPTER FIVE: To Death do us Part

The funeral of Miss Katy Lynn Mickins was held at the "On the Way to Heaven" Funeral Home on Broad Street at Lehigh Avenue because she was so well liked that her church just didn't have the capacity to hold all the people who wanted to attend. Her pastor, Bishop Thomas Lee Henderson, presided over the services and all of her children were in attendance including her oldest who was listed in the program as

"Reynolds (Noodle) Mickins." It was the saddest thing I'd ever seen in my life, made only the more so by the broken heartedness of Kala, who blamed herself for the death of Miss Mickins. She reasoned that if she hadn't "liked" Noodle as much as she did, they never would have been on that corner. "None of this would have happened," she cried late at night in our bed.

We sat on the second row across from the Mickins kids (Noodle had tried to pull her to him, but she refused). Kala, me, Brother, Sonny and Baby, had tears running free and thoughts running wild as we stared at the white coffin they'd laid her out in. Just like I was, I could tell Sonny and Brother was thinking of our parents, our lives. The death we'd experienced before felt justified, a relief from a horrific life, but this? This was a crime. Miss Mickins had never been anything but loving and kind to her kids and everybody else. But she was gone, leaving behind seven kids who had no one else, and a government house that didn't belong to them. Yes, we cried for the Mickins that day, but we also cried for ourselves and everyone else who was fighting the same fight, trying to survive in the concrete jungle.

The funeral home was packed. There was Mr. Lewis, the postman who worked from 5:00 A.M. to 5:00 P.M., Monday through Saturday. Miss Victoria who owned the beauty parlor where the Mickins girls got their hair done at least once a month (no matter how many floors their momma had to scrub to pay for it). Mr. and Mrs. Delgado from the corner store who'd sent sandwiches and sodas for the repast. And Mr. Turner who'd broke down in tears and had to close the barbershop for two days after he heard the news (a lot of little boys was happy about that). Way in the back, there was a man who people were whispering about being the father of five of the Mickins kids, but no one knew that for sure. Even Pastor Peifoy, who had been a bit insulted that he hadn't been invited to do the funeral, was sitting up front.

The Bishop Henderson preached a fine service and so many people got up to say nice things about Miss Mickins that the funeral director had to cut the line off. By the time they closed her coffin—shutting her beautiful pink gown away forever—and called for women to carry the flowers, and her sons were joined by four men from the church to carry her body from the funeral parlor to a waiting hearse, everyone was cocooned in despondency.

I followed Kala out of the church, my arm wrapped around Brother's shoulders. Poor Sonny and Baby, just about forgotten in all of this mess, followed us out to the street. Stepping out into a sun shining so high that it blinded us, we were met by whispers floating throughout the crowd, one body to another, disturbing the peace of the day. I blinked several times, adjusting my eyes, and then I saw them too. Two white men in suits, badges reflecting off the large pane windows of the funeral parlor, handcuffing Noodle as his brothers and sisters screamed and hollered and begged them not to take him away. Sassy tried to pull the back door of their car open after they stuffed him roughly inside. The unmarked police car, tires screeching against asphalt, pulled away and the back of Noodle's head disappeared in the seconds it took for the car to blend in with Broad Street traffic. So we had lost two on this saddest of days.

We were just cried out, that's why no more tears came as we walked like five broken soldiers back, toward our fortress. Kala seemed in a hurry to get there, forcing us to keep up with her hurried trot. This was hard since we all had on our Sunday shoes. But we made it back in one piece physically, if not mentally.

At home, she finally broke down, crying a storm of torrential tears. I hustled the boys off to their room with the promise of a trip to Delgado's if they played quietly for an hour. Kala had fallen into a weighty silence by the time I brewed and brought her a cup of tea. She surprised me by suddenly waving the teacup toward the floor and patting the spot next to her on the sofa to indicate that I should sit. Then she took both of my hands in hers, and began with a hoarse voice, to tell me a love story about her and Noodle.

Apparently, Miss Mickins had been sick a long time. She had an enlarged heart and needed a lot of medical attention. There had been times when she'd disappeared but I never knew or even thought about where she'd gone. It was during one of those times when she was in and out of the hospital near death, that Noodle robbed the bank. There was a special operation the doctors wanted to try on Miss Mickins but the government insurance wouldn't pay for it. Noodle robbed the bank to pay the doctors to perform the operation. They did it—then reported the large payment to the police. Miss Mickins didn't want to have the operation when she realized what Noodle had done, but her kids begged her to have it, to try to live, and she was just too weak to stand up to all of them.

"I'll risk my life, I don't care, but you are not allowed to risk yours at any time." That's what Noodle had told her a year ago. And that money had given her another year, but that's all. They said she could go at any minute, but she'd had another year to prepare her children and get her life as much in order as living where we lived allowed. I thought about my conversation with Noodle, when I'd asked him why he'd robbed that bank. Now I realized that he had to do it, to help his mother. I started crying again, my blues falling silently, watering the cracking linoleum of the living room floor.

Kala also told me how she'd cut school last week. "First and last time," she said with an I-still-can't-believe-I-did-that look on her face. Of course school had always been her salvation, even before her meeting with Jesus around the corner at the church, so my jaw dropped when she told me that.

She and Noodle had stayed home together, locked the doors and even put boards under the knobs just in case my mother decided to stop through. He had kissed her, tender, sweet, "almost as satisfying as those whiting we'd eaten the day after your father danced to death," Kala said with a sad smile.

Miss Daisy Smithfield and I had both been wrong. By the time she started circulating rumors, they had already known each other much deeper than anyone suspected. I was a little hurt that Kala hadn't told me before, but I quickly swallowed the wastefulness of self-pity as she continued the story. She told me about how Noodle's long fingers had found her breasts and she moaned in his chest as he kissed her neck, whispered lovey-dovey words into her ears. She said she could feel him, that she knew that he wanted her. It made her feel powerful and strong even though the image of his face, the touch of hands was already disappearing.

My father's face flashed before her, and Noodles long, smooth fingers suddenly felt hard and calloused. He'd rushed to remove their clothes and she stared at his tattooed back thinking how beautiful his body was against the emptiness of the room. When he'd led her towards their couch, she'd followed with *"my breath barely flowing, eyelids closing slowly to meet the red, gold and black swirling about in my mind."* She said his weight surprised her even though she had been expecting it. That it sucked the air from her lungs, making her feel as if she were drowning again in a sea of brown whiskey, and unable to control the thought of our father she'd cried out in terror. She could no longer see Noodle, the boy she thought she might one-day love, but the man who had fathered her.

"Nooo!" she'd screamed, kicking and scratching, slapping at the body that had been beautiful only a few minutes before, a curtain of shame and fear blinding her.

"Poor Noodle," she reflected, shaking her head and hiding her eyes from me because she felt ashamed. He'd jumped up, "deflated," as she called him all sorts of vile names and spat at his adulation. Then she collected her clothes from the living room floor. When the veil lifted and she was able to see Noodle again, his face was full of concern and his still-naked body was red from her punches and slaps. She fell to the floor, too shocked to speak.

"He raped you," Noodle gently observed, wrapping his shirt about her shoulders. "I'm so sorry. I'm so sorry."

"I shouldn't be telling you this," Kala said after the telling. "This is not how I wanted to tell you about sex, about what happens between a man and woman." I didn't bother to remind her that "Dallas" was my favorite TV drama, so I already had sort of a clue. "I think I fell in love with Noodle at that moment," she finished. "Not because we did it, but because we didn't."

A lot more came out over the next two weeks. A lot more happened, the most important of which was the welfare people swooped in one day like hawks and took away all of the Mickins kids. They came early in the morning, right when the sky is so deep and black that it can't help but roll over and begin again. They came like how Pastor Peifoy said Christ would come, "like thieves in the night," causing all kinds of disappearances that the world wouldn't understand. Only difference was we understood where they were going, knew it wasn't to Heaven. Kala said it was about ten DHS people, but I only saw the four that came to the front door. They brought the police, who banged on the door yelling their arrival like the entire jungle didn't already smell them.

It was trash day so sour smells pirouetted in the frosty winds. From stoops, windows, and cars, the neighborhood, which had awakened and gathered at the commotion, stared helplessly as the Mickins children were taken from our arms. Sassy, the baby girl Sweetie, Reggie, Howard and Ray were led out

127

with coats thrown quickly over their backs, scarves tied about the girls' heads, hats pressed upon the boys.' "This will kill Noodle," Kala said later when it was all over. The truth of her statement was plain enough without my agreement.

Reggie, the next to the oldest, had pulled a knife and fought. He was led in handcuffs to the station wagon they had brought for the transport. To me they looked like the Jews getting put aboard trains to concentration camps that I had seen in my history book. That gave me nightmares for about two weeks.

Kala had run out, the sleeve of her nightgown catching on the screen door with the missing screen, yelling "They can live with us! They can live with us!" One of DHS workers turned with a smirk, said "Where you going to be living at shortly?" That scared me so bad I had to run into the bathroom. When I came back to my place in the window, they were gone, the street as empty and barren as our hearts.

The next day Mrs. Smithfield's boy Frankie, who had been missing since the day he'd hit Kala with the stick and "killed" poor Miss Mickins, showed up. Rumor was that Miss Smithfield had dimed out Noodle so that her boy could come home and not worry about the Mickins kids. Came home from school and there he was, bold as a jar of spicy mustard and just as colorful in a yellow and green tweed coat. He walked up and down the streets liked he'd missed them so much that he had to soak up every nook and cranny.

We treated the Smithfields like lepers, us creatures of the concrete jungle. We ignored Mrs. Smithfield's cries for "something from the store", and her son's attempts at making jokes and his offers of cigarettes

128

and candy. Even Mr. Turner, the half-blind barber,
refused to give Frankie a haircut. They were prisoners
of our contempt, locked away with us behind brick and
mortar.

Almost two weeks after Miss Mickins died
Delgado's Grocery burnt to the ground. It was the
night of their only daughter's fifteenth birthday and
the family was away for her party. Thank God! They
had closed the store early. That ended our weekly
food allotments from Mr. Delgado. Brother topped our
list of suspects but we never spoke the words. We
just tried to watch him even closer than before. When
one of us was taking a bath, the other would step in to
keep an eye on Brother.

Noodle's court case started the following Monday,
three weeks after an uncelebrated Christmas. We
missed Noodle and his family intensely. Mr. Wilson,
who worked security at the welfare department, said
they'd all been split up and sent to different homes.
Sassy went to a shelter for girls because she was so
uncontrollable. Noodle, who had pled guilty, wrote to
Kala and asked her to attend his sentencing hearing.

"He wants to say goodbye," she bawled after
reading his letter.

My heart broke for her and myself. It felt like I
was losing a big brother. The day of the sentencing
came so quickly that we didn't have time to grieve it.
Kala allowed me to go with her (I think out of fear of
going alone) and we rode the #23 trolley downtown
and walked 2 blocks over to City Hall. My heart
breaking for Noodle, I still couldn't stop looking

around at the architecture of the building- the large courtyard with numerous entrances, the aging stature of William Penn standing erect on top. Beautiful! Even the courtroom with thick wooden brown chairs that scraped against marble when you shifted in them fascinated me.

At one o'clock, Noodle's case hadn't come up and Kala fussed in her chair knowing that the boys would have to be picked up and watched after 3:00 p.m. Finally at 1:20 p.m. Noodle entered the courtroom dressed in an orange jumpsuit, his hands cuffed in front of him. He smiled at us but his eyes were full of sorrow. This really was goodbye. I was sure bank robbery carried a heavy sentence.

"All rise," the bailiff shouted as the judge for Noodle's case approached the bench and took his seat. There was something slightly familiar about his face, his eyes, black and cold. I turned to Kala to ask her about it and to my surprise she was smiling at the judge like I had never seen her smile before.

"Don't you remember," she asked. "Look at him real good." And I did, but I still didn't see. Then it clicked: it was the strange white man who'd floated through the concrete jungle like a ghost. The man my mother had brought into our house - the man who was with Baby that awful night after the second dream. He was the judge.

His eyes skipped over us, smooth like water over flat rocks, but then they returned slowly, full of fear and something I didn't recognize. He seemed confused for a moment, but then Kala nodded toward Noodle and he gave the slightest of nods and opened a stack of files on the top of the bench. The prosecutor and public defender stood, awaiting the judge, so did Noodle. We recognized what the five fingers meant when the judge raised them under the pretense of pushing back his hair. The prosecutor asked for the maximum sentence. Kala shook her head back and forth then raised one finger. The public defender began explaining that this was Noodle's first offense and why he had robbed the bank. The Judge used three fingers to scratch the side of his face. Kala held up one - the middle finger - pretending to scratch her nose.

The mysterious man who hunted on our streets and stolen our child, sentenced Noodle to one year in prison, to be followed by seven years of probation. The prosecutor yelled, the public defender shook hands with a smiling Noodle, and we left the courtroom, our faces streaked with tears. Kala and I headed back toward the concrete jungle feeling as if we'd just slain a lion.

Four Fish

CHAPTER One – Dust to Dust

My mother was accidentally shot to death in 1981-two weeks after school let out for the summer, and close to two years after my father "accidentally" caught a pot of grits and died.   Given her lifestyle nobody was surprised but still it caught us off guard. Kala said life was like that, "It's always jumping out at you like a Jack-in-the-box. Even when you're expecting it, you still scream."

Summer roared into the city like the engine of a Hell's Angel motorcycle, hot and loud. Somebody shot President Reagan in March, but we were more concerned about who raped Mary Lewes at the Susquehanna and Dauphin subway stop. Dr. J was leading the Sixers to the Promised Land and every kid on the block had a Rubik's Cube in their pocket. The gang war between the Ministers and another gang, the Hustlers, spilled out of the night into the daylight hours. The "pop" of gunfire blended with the laughter of children, the screams of mothers, and the cursing of fathers, to create a continuous ghetto theme song in the concrete jungle. "Freebasing" cocaine became popular and the quick money drug hustlers made from their buyers took priority over anything else.

Just a week after the Mickins children were "stolen", a white family of four was moved into the house next door. Even the color of things had changed.

The night before my mother was killed Kala had dreamed of fish again, four this time, swimming in a concrete pond.

*"**It was four of them, black** as the street with little silver looking fins attached to their back. Those fish swum round and around in circles cause there wasn't nothing else they could do. After about an hour one swam fast as it could to the west edge of the pond and then it just jumped right on out. The other three fish, now knowing what to do, did the same, each taking a different direction - east, south and north."*

She'd awakened when the pond was empty.

"Well didn't they die," I asked when she recounted the dream.

"I don't know girl," she'd replied. "Couldn't see where they went but they were out, so I think they must've been happy."

"What do you think it means Kala?"

"Something is about to change." And later that day it did, just like she said it would.

When they came running, the neighbors and the police with my mother's killer in tow, I had forgotten about that dream. I think Kala had too. Just two years after my father's death, with a single shot through her left eye, my mother was finally relieved of her sad life. Mr. Henry from eight doors down and across the street on the left, cried as he told the police about catching her climbing into his bedroom window. *"I'm sorry! I didn't know it was her!"* I believed him

136

because he'd always been nice to us. But the police didn't, or just didn't care. They stuffed him in the back of the white paddy wagon with the blue trim that sat waiting for him at the curb. Jungle residents started moaning and screaming, yelling at the cops to let him go, and poor Mr. Henry was sobbing so hard that it was no way he could see out of the thick glasses hanging off his pointy nose. My heart broke for him, since it couldn't for my mother.

"Where's Sonny," Kala asked.

"Right behind me," I said turning to show her. But our little brother wasn't there.

"Sonny! Sonny, where are you boy," we cried.

"He ran down the street," Mrs. Smithfield called out from her place in the window. "Over to Henry's place I think."

Kala had to tell me what happened next 'cause she shoved me, Baby and Brother into the house and screamed at me to shut the door. She took off running after Sonny her sneakers slapping against the wet cement because the angry gray skies had chosen to open up at just that moment. About 20 minutes later the two of them came back soaked to the bone, Sonny had grease and dirt all over his shirt and pants, and Kala was wearing a warning look that said, "Don't even ask right now." But later after a few neighbors had dropped by to give their condolences and drink up our cherry Kool-Aid, and she'd finally gotten the boys settled down for the night, I heard the whole story.

Kala had found Sonny standing outside of Mr. Henry's house looking like a lost puppy. He didn't seem to notice the rain at all, though Sonny hates to be wet as much as a turtle hates to be dry. Soon they came out with my mother's body all closed up in a thick, black bag, and Sonny, he just flipped out. He tried to climb into the back of the meat wagon (the van the police used to cart away dead bodies), calling out my mother's name like he was used to her responding to his cries. It took two attendants to get him off the back of the truck although he's a skinny little thing. "It was like he was another person I'd never met before, someone out of a comic book." Kala said, shaking her damp head.

She'd wrapped him in her arms but when the meat truck pulled off real slow cause, it wasn't no need to hurry, Sonny broke away from her and ran after it calling out "Momma! Momma! Don't leave me Momma!"

That's when I knew that he'd never given up on her, that somewhere deep in his sweet little heart he'd held out some hope that one day she would be a mother to him. I cried in that moment, sad, heavy tears for our little Sonny and all of his lost dreams.

Since school was out and the free activities at the recreation center wouldn't start until the following week, we spent the morning sitting around quietly in the house. Just to keep busy I swept and mopped the kitchen and living room and Sonny, Brother and even Baby sat on the hallway steps watching my mechanical movements with big sad eyes. Kala, who had left out a couple hours before said, "We need to have respect for the dead, even if she ain't never had respect for us." She came back a few hours later with a contract in her hand.

"There ain't gonna' be no funeral. She didn't deserve it, and we ain't got the money," Kala announced. Sonny began to cry softly but we all ignored his tears. "I called Uncle Charlie like Miss Purina said when she came by. He's gonna' send just enough to the funeral home for a cremation. And that will be that." Nobody thought to ask her what a cremation was, or maybe we just didn't want to know. I did want to know about Uncle Charlie but thought it wise to save my questions until later when the "children" were in bed. After fixing us tuna fish sandwiches and pouring cold glasses of milk (I was still mad about our Kool-Aid), she sent us outside to sit in the sun saying, "Y'all look mighty dry today. Go on outside and get some sweat on you." But I knew she just needed some time to be alone.

Early Friday morning - my mother was about four days dead then - Kala woke us up right after the sun came up over top of the big Center City buildings, and told us get dressed for our mother's funeral services. My eyes were so heavy with sleepiness that I ran face first into the edge of the door and developed a big hickey on the side of my head. "Just get dressed," my big sister hissed when I complained about the pain. We wore black and blue, stripes and plaid, whatever counted as a nice outfit to say goodbye. The funeral director had agreed to say something over our mother for free if we got there by 8:00 A.M. He had two funerals that day.

139

We found out quickly enough about cremation when we stared at what was left of our mother in a brown clay urn. She had been burned down to nothing. I was furious with Kala. Nobody, no matter how mean they were should be burnt up so that you couldn't get one last look at their face if you wanted. Sonny felt the same way. He rushed off to the bathroom so that he didn't vomit on his clothes. When he came back he picked up the urn and placed it gentle like against his Vaseline moisten lips leaving a greasy lip stain right in the middle of the clay jar. Brother even lost his tough exterior for a few minutes and shed a tear.

"That's dirt," Baby cried out.

He always was the one to tell the truth even when you didn't want him to. I plucked him in the back of his head when Kala wasn't looking and gave him a warning glance not to say anything. The Funeral Director said a few words that were meaningless to us and rushed us out of there.

It wasn't a long walk home, but Kala said we were taking the bus. I figured it was her way of trying to make us feel better since we rarely got to ride. But a block into the ride, which we spent with our faces, flattened against smudged glass, she revealed her plan to us.

"We leaving her right here," she announced to no one in particular. "If you got any goodbyes, say them now. Our stop is coming up." Nobody moved, not even Sonny.

Silently we departed the #3 bus leaving the urn on the back seat. My mother had never escaped the concrete jungle; we figured she would enjoy touring the city in her afterlife. Besides, nobody wanted that dirt in the bottle to come home with us.

CHAPTER TWO – Aunt Charlie

Summer was fully upon us and Kala was working days at The Dip, a greasy spoon restaurant on the Avenue, and nights and weekends at her job downtown. This meant we were stuck in the hot house a lot. I kept thinking my mother would show up and try to take the new television Kala had purchased from the Goodwill, or fight with her because she'd spent the food stamps. The wooden boards we'd used to secure the doorknobs sat unused in the corners behind the front and back doors and I even wondered if we should just toss them out.

Sonny fell into what we later realized was a deep depression. He stayed locked up in his room most days and hardly talked to us at all. I caught Brother lighting a book of matches in the bathroom and slapped him real hard across the face. From the cold look in his eyes I knew that he wouldn't stop. Our phone was shut off again so to communicate with friends or passersby I hung out of the living room window. It was a miserable, lonely summer and 'though I knew Kala was killing herself to take care of us I was still angry at being left in charge day and night.

Kala was worried sick that the Welfare people would come and send us away to different places like they had done to the Mickins kids. The only income we had coming in was from her low-paying jobs and she was considering dropping out of school for something full-time that paid more money. What she made wasn't enough, but somehow she made it work week after week.

The lady who ran the rental office of Fairhill Projects, Mrs. Marshall came past every week. Kala told us to "Never talk to her. You get on inside if she tries to talk to you." She was always on guard, and it made her appear older than her sixteen16 years. I wanted to tell her that she was starting be just as mean as our mother and father, but I knew she would be hurt if I did, so I didn't.

Just when I thought it would be the most miserable summer ever, one of the best things of our lives occurred. It was one of those rare Saturdays when Kala had off from work. Throw pillow beneath her for comfort, she watched us like a hawk from her place on the stoop.   Brother and Sonny were down on their knees studying a family of ants that were trying to drag a piece of peppermint into a crack. They looked up every few minutes to make sure that she hadn't moved. The boys were still total opposites but had insects in common.

Baby sat cuddled in her lap, licking on an orange Popsicle and dribbling sweet juices down his chin. Kala was fussing about how he needed a haircut, how all the boys did, and she threatened Sonny and Brother, "If you kill them ants I'm gonna' cut your hair myself." I was playing Double Dutch and in between my turns she waved at me and I blew her kisses. It was good to have her home, good to be outside. I savored it because I knew the late afternoon fun would be over soon, that she would shoo us in for a cold dinner of bologna and cheese sandwiches and cool baths before she left for her night job.

Thirty-two days after my mother began her eternal bus ride, our Uncle Charlie who was just a helpful memory to us, came up from Georgia to pay his respects and never left. Kala was the only one who wasn't surprised by it. She reasoned, "Just when you ain't expecting a thing, that's when that thing is expecting you". I still can't figure out what she was talking about, finally gave up after giving myself a headache thinking about it for a long time.

My momma and your momma was sitting in a tree... Childish voices rang out around me as I jumped fast, with eyes closed, in between those two plastic-coated laundry ropes. A misstep would not only mean the loss of my turn, but the possibility of a quick-rising whelp on my exposed legs. *My momma told your momma – get away from me.* I raised my elbows and picked up my knees. I imagined I could jump all night without getting winded in the least. I was good at this, unstoppable, until the rope stopped suddenly, falling without fanfare or advance notice. I was shocked, and more than a little bit angry - opened my eyes to confront my rope turners, smart remark on my lips.

Then I heard, "Child, is that you?"

The question froze my words in my mouth and I stopped dead in my tracks.

There she was. The largest woman I'd ever seen opening the door of the most amazing car - a 1973 Mustang - I found out later. She stepped out right in front of our house and stretched her huge arms and hands toward the setting sun. Her bright red fingernails glittered like rubies.

"Sure was a long drive," she announced. With our mouths wide open, we watched her shake her long, waist-length hair from side to side, then march her three-inch patent leather pumps right up to Kala. Her face reminded me so much of my mother that I shivered thinking it her ghost. "Well ain't that a beautiful baby," she laughed extending her well manicure hand. "My name is Charlie. You the niece that called?"

"Aunt--I mean Uncle Charlie? Is it you?" Kala stammered shocked by his thick muscular thighs covered in red sheer nylons that exploded beneath a stylish black and white stripe mini skirt. His red halter-top held up by Lord knows what, tied the outfit all together.

"In the flesh baby girl," he said with a deep laugh. "It's your Aunt Charlie."

As soon as the boys, who had reared up and were ready to pounce if necessary, heard that this was their uncle/aunt they charged for his car.

"Let us have a ride," they shouted in unison.

Kala was up fast, Baby still holding on to her neck for dear life, like a crab. She grabbed them by the back of their tee shirts demanding, "Show your manners!"

But it *was* a beautiful car and we all stared at it in awe. Apple red with silver leather interior and black trim, it was a made for riding. We all rubbed our dirty hands on the shiny finish leaving prints everywhere, but Charlie didn't complain a bit. Kala stared at the car, at our smiling-wide Uncle/Aunt Charlie, and began to cry. She did that a lot now that my father and mother were both gone. The boys became frightened and gathered around her protectively. But I followed her eyes until mine landed where hers were focused. Hanging from the rearview mirror, swinging gently in the warm summer breeze, were four tiny little black stuffed fish. They had traveled a long way with Aunt Charlie.

When Kala had dreamed of the fish in the concrete pond she knew it meant change but didn't know for sure how it was going to come. Well Aunt Charlie was certainly a change, I thought with a big smile. He retrieved a worn duffle bag and slung it easily over his wide shoulders. "Well baby girl, you gonna' let me in or what?" he asked with a big booming laugh as he switched through the crowd of stunned faces. "I don't need much room, although you can't tell from the size of me. Just a little space until I get settled."

Later that night Kala told me that she wasn't sure why'd she trusted him, but she did and for once she didn't have to yell to get us to come into the house. We couldn't wait to see what Aunt Charlie had to say. Happy to oblige, he flopped down on the couch, kicked off his shoes and crossed his legs.

"Where you'd come from," Brother asked standing in from of him in a bold stance.

145

"You got a lot of gumption boy," Aunt Charlie laughed. "If you get me a cold glass of water I might just oblige your question."

Aunt Charlie spent the next hour talking non-stop about family members we had never met and places we had never seen. We had never met anyone like Charlie before and we stared even though Kala said it rude to do so. I looked over and saw her staring too, so I knew Charlie was something special 'cause very few things caught her by surprise. When he spoke, his voice was full of laughter and fun, and he used his hands to emphasis his words. Baby kept calling him "momma" which caused everybody but Kala to crack up.

A hairdresser by trade, within an hour he'd cut all of the boys' heads and greased and braided mine into cute African twists that no one else had ever seen before. Kala finally relented after some protest to a hard press. I was shocked to see her hair extend well beyond her shoulders. We all looked so spit-shine clean that Kala decided to run next door, call out of work, and spend some of our precious money on a late movie for everyone. On the way out the door Sonny, the family scientist, asked the question that we all had been dying to ask since the moment Charlie stepped from the car.

"So what are you?" Everybody froze, our bodies rigid with tension, as we waited for an answer.

"Well, I guess some people would call me a faggot, or a fairy if they wanted to be nice, but I just call myself Miss Charlie," he replied with a serious look on his face. "God don't love me no more or no less 'cause I like to wear dresses instead of pants and I've ran from that fact for far too much of my life. I want y'all to know right now, that I'm not running from myself coming here to see you. I'm running to family, and I'm bringing love." He paused, stopping to look each of us in the eye. I appreciated that most about what he said. "I hope that's okay with you."

Each of us nodded yes, with smiles on our faces. Nobody but Kala had ever offered us such a gift before.

Like old friends we piled into Aunt Charlie's beautiful Mustang that he had driven all the way from Georgia, waving proudly at the nosy neighbors who watched opened mouthed through their screen doors. Kala said at that very moment she'd decided – Aunt/Uncle Charlie could definitely stay around for a while. After the movie, we came back to a busy block. White light bulbs surround by flies and mosquitoes shined dimly over most of the porches, except for the Wheatfields who kept different colored bulbs in their outdoor light. Concrete jungle kids ran back and forth on cooling sidewalks as music blasted from open doors and teenagers hung out on the corners jonsing with each other. I spotted three girls from my middle school class running from a pack of boys yelling "catch a girl - get a girl." I waved proudly to Ricky Wheatfield who stared with an open mouth as Aunt Charlie parked in front of our front door. I could tell the tongues had been wagging while were gone with everybody wanting to know who our visitor was, but we ignored their questioning looks as we marched like soldiers back into our house.

147

CHAPTER THREE - Throwing out the Baby with the Bath Water

First thing Charlie did when he went up to the second floor was ask why two bedrooms were locked and nobody was using them. All four bedrooms and the single bath created a pentagon, so we had to walk past the closed off ones every day, but we had grown so used seeing the doors closed that we forgot that they had the ability to open. We hadn't even thought about the "empty room" since Miss Purina's visit, and nobody even thought about taking the room our mother and father had shared. We had been perfectly content to continue sharing beds and rooms. When no one answered Aunt Charlie's question he looked back and forth from one curious face to another until Brother finally said, as cocky as he pleased, "They killed the grandmother we never knew in that room, and the other one belonged to our mother and father, the killers." In the dull yellow light of the small hallway, the four of us shifted from leg to leg, the wonderful night coming to a close with confusion and embarrassment.

"Shut up Brother!" Kala warned, pinching the fleshy back of his arm. "Don't say stuff like that, especially in front of Baby." Sonny looked like he was going to be sick and I stepped away from him hoping to avoid any sudden bodily spills.

"Aaah," Aunt Charlie replied, like he suddenly understood what he never had. "Well I say it's time to throw the baby out with the bath water."

"Baby don't want to go out," Baby whined, and Charlie laughed.

"You can sleep on the couch for now Aunt Charlie," Kala volunteered, a hesitant look in her eye. "We can figure something out later. I'm sorry since I didn't know you were coming I wasn't thinking about sleeping arrangements."

"Nonsense honey. If there are two empty rooms why would I do that? Let's just open up these doors and see what we got to work with."

"No!" Kala's shouting stunned us all and we looked at her like she had two heads or something. "No, I don't think you should do that Aunt Charlie." I stared at her curiously. She pretended not to notice.

Aunt Charlie smiled at her patiently, and reached out to take one of her hands into his. Surprisingly she let him do it. "Kala baby why don't you let the kids go on down and watch some television? I want to have a little talk with you." She nodded and we solemnly piled down the stairs, four heads bobbing to the beat of change.

An hour later they called us up for baths and bed. A newly flat-chested Aunt Charlie—who had changed into a fluffy pink robe with matching slippers— carefully picked up Baby and held him in his arms like an infant. It was so sweet, so loving, that I wanted to cry from the yearning I felt to have him do the same for me. In that moment, walking up the stairs behind them, I missed my mother, even though she had never really mothered me. Kala must have

149

noticed the look in my eyes 'cause she grabbed my hand and squeezed it real tight. Aunt Charlie laid Baby on the bed, pulled off his sneakers, and covered him. We watched open-mouthed as he disappeared into the room that had once been our parents. Brother and Sonny didn't bathe together any more so they took turns in the bathroom while I waited patiently. That's when Kala told me what Aunt Charlie meant by "throwing out the baby with the bath water."

Stretched out across the bed we stared wide eyed at the fat, white moon as she talked. "Charlie said we can't keep living our lives behind closed doors. He said sometimes we got to stop and re-evaluate what to keep in our hearts and what to throw out."

"What'd he mean by that?" I interrupted.

"Well if you let me tell you, I will. I swear girl you're allows making me lose my train of thought." But she was smiling so I knew it was alright to continue the joke.

"Where do you think your train of thought went this time Kala?"

"Girl, I don't know - New York, Chicago, China- anywhere but right here, right now." Then we giggled together which was my favorite thing in the world to do with her.

"So you want to hear the rest of it or not?" she asked, but then continued without waiting to hear my answer.

"Aunt Charlie opened the doors, both of them, and you know what? There wasn't nothing in there but some old furniture and stuff and an awful smell from them being closed off so long." Her eyes turned toward the ceiling where the long shadow from the dresser spread out in a rectangular shape. "He put my hand on those doorknobs and asked me to turn them. He said that since I had been the keeper of their secrets for so long, it wouldn't be right for him to take that from me." A smile tugged slightly at the corner of her dark lips. "It did feel good though, opening those doors that I had forgotten even existed. When he opened up our grandmom's room, I could still smell her, just a bit. Then it was gone like a fart in a cool breeze. Jean Naté, that's what I think I smelled.

"Hmm, I like Jean Naté," I murmured, then paused to listen to Brother yelling for Sonny to get out of the bathroom.

"What's that throwing the baby out thing though?" My stomach rumbled from all of the popcorn and soda I'd eaten at the movie theater where we saw a Bill Cosby and Sidney Poitier comedy that split our sides with laughter

"Well, Aunt Charlie told me how folks are always saying, 'Don't make the mistake of throwing out something important when you're trying to throw out what you don't want no more. But sometimes the only way to get rid of what's really eating at your soul is to toss out the whole thing."

"That sounds crazy to me Kala. If something is important, shouldn't you hold on to as hard as you can?" I asked, sitting up to pull off my shirt. (Brother had finally gotten in the bathroom so it wouldn't be long before my turn). "Why you listening so hard to him—I mean her—oh you know what I mean."

"I don't know for sure," Kala replied. "Maybe I'm just tired. Or maybe it was that money he sent to cremate your mother. But he is right, holding on to stuff don't leave no room for the new. If I didn't open those doors Aunt Charlie wouldn't be able to stay with us. Besides, my dream about the fish said it was going to be change coming."

I nodded 'cause what she said made sense plus I had to pee and needed her to stop talking. Then I remembered what I wanted to ask: Well, what's going to happen with the other room?" And this time she just nodded and smiled.

CHAPTER FOUR - Dog Food

Aunt Charlie's place in our hearts was solidified by two events that took place within a month of each other. The first incident happened just one day after his arrival. We woke to foreign smells floating upstairs like butterfly wings from the kitchen. Kala was still lying beside me so I knew that she wasn't the source of them. The steady growl in my belly kept me from pondering for too long.

Apparently Brother, Sonny and Baby had the same idea. On my way to the bathroom, I saw them standing around with crumbs of sleep in their eyes, sniffing the air like they were still dreaming. My footsteps sounded hollow as I walked down the steps alone. Peering into the kitchen my eyes fell first on Aunt Charlie, fully dressed in pink satin slacks and a white cotton shirt, damp from the sweat running down his long back. He turned to face me with a white toothy smile.

"Well, I was wondering who would be the first one down for my breakfast," he said with a chuckle. His voice sounded so close to my mother's that it ached for me to hold a smile on my face. "I'm famous all over the South for my breakfasts, you know."

"And I believe it," I said, happily sliding into my chair at the round kitchen table loaded with all kinds of steaming foods. Butter dripped slowly down a fat, fluffy stack of pancakes. Still-sizzling bacon was spread out on grandmom's good platter next to a large mountain of scrambled eggs. To the right was another plate, this one full of plump pork sausage, fried potatoes, and almost-burned-to-a-crisp scrapple.

"This was my momma's plate," he said, pointing to one of the platters. I nodded, pinching my thigh under the table to see if I was dreaming.

"I didn't know what y'all like, so I went to the supermarket up the road this morning and bought it all," he said of the feast, his eyes glowing in the bright kitchen sunlight. "Truth be told, and I always try to tell it little girl, that drive up here left me feeling pretty hungry myself."

Living in a house without parents can sometimes create loose lips in a person. I found myself asking, "But where'd you get the money?" as if Aunt Charlie wasn't good enough, smart enough, or just *enough* to have the ability to purchase a bag of groceries. I immediately felt I had insulted him and wanted to apologize, although I didn't know how or why. He took the chair beside me, his head shaking with a heavy sadness.

"Girl, my sister and that bum of a husband of hers did wrong by y'all kids, but as long as Aunt Charlie is around you won't ever starve," he said, taking my hand. I couldn't help myself; I began to cry, my tears bathing his large, warm hand.

"Oh chile' hush now," he whispered. "I make the best pancakes in the world. They make anything feel better."

Half an hour later, our stomachs bursting like those little starving kids on the *Save the Children* commercials, we all agreed that he had been telling the truth. It was the best meal we'd ever eaten, and even Kala begrudgingly agreed, though I know she was a little jealous of our appreciation of Aunt Charlie's cooking. We were still at the table, swinging our legs back and forth with satisfaction, talking loudly as we vied for Aunt Charlie's attention, when Mrs. Kelly, the lady from the project's rental office, banged on the back door. Brother and Sonny took off upstairs like we'd been taught. I grabbed Baby's hand and half dragged him 'cause he didn't want to leave the table. That left Kala and Aunt Charlie to face Mrs. Kelly.

Later, Kala described how Aunt Charlie had yanked the back door open before she had a chance to stop him.

"Help you?" he asked Mrs. Kelly, leaving off the "Can I."

"Who are you?" she stammered, clearly as shocked by Aunt Charlie's appearance as we were yesterday when he stepped out of his pretty red car full of love and surprises.

"Charlie Benson, but you can call me Miss Charlie if you want. C'mon in here, honey chile'," he replied holding the door wide for the person we'd been trying to avoid for a month now. "Whew girl you look hungry."

To say that Mrs. Kelly was a bit thin would be a gross understatement. Pinky told me once that she never eats, somebody else said she does eat, she just don't swallow. But her nephew Kyle, a nice boy who had come to live with her from Ohio, said she eats a whole bunch of food then throws it all up, sometimes in jars and buckets that Mr. Kelly finds in the most surprising ways. He raised the roof about it once, tossing and breaking bottles full of vomit so that the entire apartment stunk to high heaven. That's what he said, exactly. After that Mr. Kelly just started hanging out with other women and drinking a lot.

"So Mr. Benson..."

"Miss Charlie," he interrupted. "Call me Miss Charlie."

"Welfare's coming for these kids on Friday. They need to be packed and ready by then," Mrs. Kelly stuttered as Aunt Charlie pulled out a chair and waved for her to sit.

"Have a seat honey," Charlie said with a large smile. "Now tell me again exactly how much these children owe you Mrs. Kelly."

"Oh this ain't about the money," the rental office lady claimed. Kala said she wanted slap the lie out of her mouth like my father was always promising to do to us, but instead she rolled her eyes and shot mental daggers her way. "It's my duty, working for the state and city and all, to make sure these poor children are under adult supervision." And then, as an after-thought she added, "Sorry 'bout your loss too, umm, Miss Charlie."

Later, as we hung our tub-washed clothes in the backyard and Kala repeated the conversation, she had me laughing so hard that I had to hold on to the clothesline to keep from tumbling into the dirt.

"Why don't you sit and have something to eat?" Aunt Charlie had offered Mrs. Kelly, ignoring how Kala was shaking her head no like crazy. "We got plenty left." And we did, so it wasn't a lie.

"The rent is *paid*," Kala had stated proudly. "We don't owe her nothing, Aunt Charlie."

"They still gotta' go though. It's my duty to report orphans to the welfare department," Mrs. Kelly muttered as Aunt Charlie placed a stack of pancakes and two pork sausages in front of her. "I could lose my job, you know."

"Of course, I understand," Aunt Charlie said. "But ain't no orphans here, honey. These kids got family—me—and I'm going to be right here taking care of this house." Thick, rich Alaga Syrup dripped from the bottle he held over her plate. "Ain't nothing to worry about here. Nope, nothing at all."

Kala didn't know who was more shocked by his words, Aunt Charlie, her or Mrs. Kelly, who ravenously attacked the stack of pancakes, then asked for seconds. After breakfast, she left with a hair appointment (Aunt Charlie wanted to work on her dry roots) for the next afternoon and three sausage links wrapped tight in a paper napkin. *Poor Mr. Kelly*, I thought. He was sure to be finding some vomit-filled jars tonight.

Over the next three weeks, we melted into a summer heat wave like icing on a hot cake. Orange water plugs spewed thousands of gallons of city water into the streets forcing residents to run to their bathtubs early in the morning if they wanted to wash their clothes or their behinds. The Good Humor truck took up a permanent parking spot on the corner, and we spent more time begging the driver for a red, white and blue Bomb Pop than watching *Green Acres* reruns on our new color television set. Jungle people walked, ran, sat, talked, fought, made up, laughed, lived. Brown, black and beige women wore pink, purple, yellow and green polyester shorts, halter-tops and sundresses. Kids danced wildly under makeshift waterfalls, threatening passing cars with buckets of water. Overheated drunks fell over on their neighbors steps. Flip Flops slapped against the concrete as we jumped up and down for hours singing made up songs about nothing—"Challenge, Challenge, one, two, three, four, five."

Shirts and shorts clung to heated skin like fitted sheets to a mattress. Afros tightened into knotty bushes, and the smell of hot combs and Dixie Peach filled the humid evening air as people prepared for the next house party. In the evenings, we watched teen girls jiggling in their tube tops, Calvins and platform sandals, and the boys stepping out in loud shirts and Bell, Biv, Devoe haircuts decorated with intricate parts. At least two days a week we woke to the horrible smell of bleach and the husky cuss words of Aunt Charlie who was in constant battle with the maggots that invaded our backyard trashcans. The '80s were in full swing, and Donna Summer ruled the airways. Concrete jungle people suffered happily.

Aunt Charlie's presence provided Kala with a new freedom. It scared her I think, making her temper as hot as the weather. My brothers and I often rushed to the park, the community center, or the library to get away from her evilness and sudden fits of anger. Aunt Charlie, on the other hand, remained kind and civil, making room for her sullen attitude and her "tiny little growth spurts." as he called them.   They agreed that he would work out of the house during the day, while she worked nights at her cleaning job in Center City.

I was constantly afraid that Aunt Charlie would leave us. Young boys taunted him with "faggot, faggot, faggot," and his beautiful red car was attacked by eggs and scratched with foreign objects in the middle of the night. Sonny and Brother were teased unmercifully and told they would become "faggots" too, but nothing they did ran Aunt Charlie away.

After the second week, when the blatant harassment had died down to barroom and front-step gossip, I finally asked him why he didn't just jump back in his car and escape from the jungle before he got cemented in. He just laughed and said, "Girl, one of the worst lives there is chose me and I'm living it as hard and fast as I can. See, a lot of people hate me just for the adrenaline rush they get from doing so. I decided early on that if I let that hate determine what kind of life I'm going to live, then I may as well have stayed in that hole my daddy buried me in a long time ago on the farm." Then he just walked away without answering any of my questions about the farm and his daddy.

By the third week of summer, word of Uncle Charlie's hair skills had spread throughout the concrete jungle and he rapidly built up a steady stream of customers. Women sat around our kitchen table waiting for their turn to be curled, permed or braided, all the while laughing at his jokes, and nibbling on squares of his fresh-baked cornbread. With the money Aunt Charlie contributed and Kala's wages, we were able to have the phone line restored and began to replace some household items that had gone unexplainably missing in the months before Aunt Charlie arrived. Charlie seemed to have room in his heart for everybody, and every one of his customers felt special when they left. A few men even snuck in for haircuts after sundown.

"Why do you keep laughing and joking with those people when you know they talk behind your back," Kala asked him one evening after his last customer had gone.

"Chile' you got to be nice to everybody. God tells you that," he replied, then sat down to rub his sore feet. "Whew, them women came a calling today— every one of them wanting something different."

Kala shook her head.

"You ought to let me do something with your head tomorrow. You're my niece and you're walking around here looking like a frightened chick."

"My hair is fine!" Kala shouted, suddenly angry.

"So you're mad now?" Aunt Charlie asked incredulously. "Don't you know all the anger inside of you is hurtful?" He laughed softly then added, "Being angry at people is like you drinking a whole bottle of lye and expecting the other person to die. It eats at you something awful."

Not knowing what to say, she kept quiet.

"It's a hateful world out here Kala, but it's what you make of it. Why don't you get you a boyfriend, go out some time girl?"

Her tears came before she had a chance to stop them. Aunt Charlie, knowing she needed it, let her cry, pushing the little ones out of the kitchen when they came to investigate their big sister's sobs. When the flood subsided, he wrapped his big arms around her. His sweet funk filled her nostrils, and she giggled imagining him spraying on perfume.

"Now what's so funny?" Aunt Charlie asked.

"You smell like perfume," she said, sniffling and then hiding a smile behind her hand. He burst into laughter and pulled her close for another long hug. After that Kala softened a bit toward Aunt Charlie, but it wasn't until he saved Brother from the Ministers' Doberman Pinchers that she just gave up and started loving him fully.

While Sonny wore his grief on his sleeve, Brother hid his pain behind a mask of jokes and misbehavior. Determined to get back at the Ministers for supplying drugs to my mother, Brother had begun a small sabotage campaign against them, tossing Molotov cocktails at their cars in the middle of the night. (The boy actually used sheets to sneak out of his second story bedroom window.) He also left stink bombs on the steps of their drug houses, and threw rocks from the roof at their drug runners as customers approached. He was at war, fighting singlehandedly against one of the most dangerous gangs in North Philly.

Thirty days after Aunt Charlie arrived—I'd been counting by making big red Xs on the wall calendar—all hell broke loose on 10th Street. It was late afternoon, but still too early for a summertime dinner. Kala and I sat cross-legged on the stoop playing a game of Miss Mary Mack.

Miss Mary Mack, Mack Mack, all dressed in Black, Black, Black, with silver buttons, buttons, buttons, all down her back, back, back.

She had the night off and Aunt Charlie decided it was time for his first night out in the big city. Baby's laughter floated out of the screen door with the missing screen (Aunt Charlie was in a running debate with project housing about fixing the door) as he enjoyed some comedic act on television. Sonny, as usual, had locked himself away in his room to perform some kind of science experiment with the science kit Kala found for him at the thrift store. (Brother said he was looking at his sperm under the microscope.)

161

Brother spent most of his free time at the new recreation center two blocks away.

Our first Fourth of July with Aunt Charlie had passed three weeks prior but symbols of patriotism continued to drape some of the windows of the residents of the concrete jungle. Wrinkled flags hung lifelessly on the sills of open windows as the community hung stubbornly on to the memory of barbeque, fireworks, and Pinky and his girlfriend Rhonda running naked down the street. His mother caught them "doing the nasty" on the kitchen table right next to her bowl of church picnic potato salad and she went after him with a butcher's knife. He ran outside with his albino penis flapping between his legs and bits of onions, green pepper and celery littering the sidewalk. Mrs. Smithfield waved from her post but Kala rolled her eyes and I licked out my tongue. Noodle rarely wrote, but he was still deeply engrained in our hearts. Across the street a little boy sat crying in Mr. Turner's barbershop chair as Miss Ida stopped long enough on her trek to the Avenue to look us up and down.

"What y'all doing?" she demanded, like she couldn't see us playing Miss Mary Mack.

Kala still couldn't stand her, but I gave her a slight smile before turning away. Aunt Charlie had taken to doing her hair and we knew she really wanted to see if he were home, but neither one of us would volunteer the information.

"Charlie home?" she finally asked.

"Nope," we said in unison.

Miss Ida stood there for a minute like we were going to change our minds, then moved on down to the corner to gossip with the Jehovah Witness lady who spent half of her life escaping slamming front doors. With our hands moving faster than our brains we continued the mindless game. Then we heard him coming, moving fast like the subway train and with almost as much noise. "Run!" he screamed turning the corner so quickly that Miss Ida had to jump back to keep from being knocked over. "Run!"

Of course Kala and I froze at the sight of him. Patches of violet blood streaked his white tee shirt, a large tear separated the knee of his pants, and his face looked swollen two sizes too large. It was Brother—who else could it be?

Not 30 seconds after he turned that corner, two black and brown Doberman Pinchers followed, their teeth bared for biting and their tails clipped for balance. Brother ran toward the front door, dogs on his heels, as we watched shocked and helpless. In the second it took to think the thought, I knew he would never make it inside the house. My bladder sent hot pee rushing down my shorts, drenching my ankles. Our screams created a soliloquy (I won the spelling bee with this one) of terror. Then, out of the corner of my eye, I caught a streak of muscled black and brown. The dogs had charged the stoop. I could see bodies moving with what looked to me like the speed of light.

My eyes and Kala's locked dark brown to light, as our heads turned in the direction of Brother and the two dogs. He had fallen at the top step, right in front of the screen door, a vicious wail flowing like a bad horn's from his trembling lips. Suddenly, the leader of the two dogs was airborne, his long, thin body graceful and deadly. But before his dripping fangs could connect with Brother's arm, the screen door with the missing screen slammed into his canine visage with the power of a cannon blast. He fell breathlessly, as stunned by the collision as we were.

The second dog leaped next, only to be caught by a huge brown hand and a wall of blinding yellow. It was Uncle Charlie, dressed to the nines in a bright yellow sundress, yellow high-heeled sandals, and a floppy straw hat decorated with a large yellow and white bow. He held the second dog by his broken neck with one hand and reached out to Brother with the other. The other dog lay unconscious at Aunt Charlie's beautifully manicured feet.

"What the hell is going on here?" he roared. "If you all didn't want me to go out all you had to do was say it."

We would have laughed then, I'm sure of it, if three young men dressed in black jeans, white tee shirts, and black berets hadn't come from the same direction as Brother and the Dobermans - the Ministers. I would have peed myself if I wasn't already wet.

"What'd you do to my dog?" one of them whined.

"This yours," Aunt Charlie asked with little concern. "Must have gotten loose - tried to attack my nephew."

"'Supposed to attack him after what he done," the biggest one of the group shot back. "What the hell are you anyway? How'd you kill that dog?"

"You killed my mother!" Brother yelled, an accusing finger pointing in their direction. "You sold her drugs and made her do ugly stuff to get them!"

Kala puffed up like the Pillsbury Dough Boy and marched right over and slapped him clean across the face. He stared at her defiantly for a moment then burst into tears, which in turn made her pull him close in her arms. "Boy, your momma was a drug addict and a whore. Don't you go getting us killed over her," she said softly, wiping his tears with the back of her hand. Baby stood in the doorway, snot running out his nose, his face in the place where the screen should be in the door.

"I didn't do nothin'," Brother insisted, just as Sonny's head appeared in the second floor window with a glass beaker in his hand. He appeared to be ready to drop it if necessary.

"Trouble don't be where trouble ain't at," Aunt Charlie replied.

I could hear the heavy squeaking of concrete jungle doors opening. Now that the immediate danger was over I wanted to get into the house before the entire neighborhood saw my wet shorts. Unfortunately, my pathway was blocked by Aunt Charlie, Kala, Brother and the dude from the Ministers. I tried to signal Kala to get me in the house, but she was distracted by the melee.

Aunt Charlie tossed the dead dog and he landed with a thud in front of his owner. "Take your trash and get out of here man." By this time, the first dog had stumbled to his feet, dazed, and a different animal. He attempted a growl but it came out more like a sick moan.

"Spade! Spade! Come here, boy," the first gang member called. "Come here, boy." Then he turned to Aunt Charlie and declared, "I'm going to kill you for this!"

A knife appeared suddenly, its blade glinting dangerously in the sun. He charged without thought or caution, swinging wildly with the weapon. Aunt Charlie stepped out of the way, and then slapped him hard across the face (now I knew where Kala got it from), drawing blood and rage as the boy lunged again. "I don't want to hurt you, but I will if you make me," Aunt Charlie promised, gripping the boy's offending arm. "I have eight years of the Marines under my belt, and I can kill a man a hundred different ways. But I don't want to kill you unless you make me."

Our mouths fell open in shock. "Now, go on man. I promise you the boy won't be bothering you again."

"Come on T-Bone, get your dog man and just come on," a third gangster called out. "I don't even want to explain how a faggot kicked your little skinny ass." Aunt Charlie dropped T-Bone's arm, and the boy picked up his dead dog and called the other. Man and dog limped away together, their eyes full of revenge.

CHAPTER FIVE - Seasons

Summer swept by quickly. In the cool fall breeze empty cigarette packs and beers cans moved up and down the streets. The launch of the space shuttle Columbia was still the biggest story on the evening news, and drive-by shootings were becoming popular. Mrs. Smithfield's son Frankie was shot dead outside the Dew Drop Inn for trying to sell a $5 bag of weed on the corner. We saw her entire body (surprisingly, she looked perfectly normal) when Aunt Charlie did her hair for her only son's funeral. We didn't attend the services, but Aunt Charlie did make her a macaroni and cheese casserole and made me take it to her.

The senseless murders of 28 little kids in Atlanta had jungle parents' on edge and they kept a closer watch on their children as they ended the last of the summer evenings out on their stoops. Even though Baby finally stopped wetting the bed even though he still occasionally stood up in the middle of night and peed on Sonny and Brother thinking he was in the bathroom. With Aunt Charlie in the house, school preparations went smoothly for the first time. New clothes, book bags and lunch boxes were purchased three weeks before school started and we were all excited to go back. Brother had been repentant for the rest of summer, spending most of his time buried in a book, even taking barber lessons from Aunt Charlie. But the biggest news involved Kala and the opportunity of lifetime.

Since Aunt Charlie listed himself as our guardian on school records, he was the one notified about Kala's scholarship award to St. Peter's Christian Academy, the most prestige private school in Philadelphia. Nominated by her 9th grade principal at Kensington High School, it was an honor very few African American students ever received and would mean she would have to study extra hours to keep up and quit her janitorial job. Kala was terrified, and mad as hell that he had accepted the invitation.

Aunt Charlie wasn't having none of it. "Chile, you don't have the right to throw away opportunity!" he shouted. For the first time he appeared angry about something. "People died, got bit by dogs and walked to work for a year for you to go to a school like this." Running his huge hands through his graying hair, he paced back and forth, his chest heaving with rage.

"What if I can't compete?" Kala mumbled.

"Compete? Girl you already done won," he said, lifting her head with the tip of his finger. "Only way you can lose now is to blow this chance. Humph, I wish I had a chance, that I didn't have the life they gave me."

It was rare for Aunt Charlie to discuss his past and the comment immediately caught her interest, but Kala had taken a stand and didn't want to back down. "I like it where I am, and that's where I'm gonna' stay," she said defiantly, sucking her teeth and rolling her eyes. "You ain't my father."

"Which you should thank God for," Aunt Charlie threw at her viciously, though I saw regret fill his eyes the moment he said the words.

168

Her face cracked with hurt as she stomped out of the room, locking herself in the bathroom until Sonny screamed and hollered with pain from needing to go. Across seas, thousands of miles away, President Reagan was beginning a political battle to tear down a wall (I read that in one of the local papers) that had been built decades before. Meanwhile, right in our house, another wall made of stubbornness and hurt was going up. A cold war had begun.

For days thick tension filled the air and they avoided each other as much as possible. Aunt Charlie wasn't speaking to Kala, and she hid her fear behind a blockade of anger. They spent the next week slamming doors, stomping floors and yelling at us kids for no good reason. Charlie's customers who didn't have sense enough not to ask "What's going on" were punished by his sizzling hot curling irons and his cold looks - that stopped the questions. I could tell Kala missed their afternoon banter because I caught her sitting at the top of the stairs listening to the neighborhood gossip and storytelling several times.

"Miss Fine, if you don't hold still you're going to end up with half your head sloped."

"Sorry Miss Charlie." And then laughter erupted around the kitchen as everyone remembered the old tuna fish commercial. "But girl, this is what gossip was invented for."

"Go on Ida, finish the story," yelled out another one of Aunt Charlie's customers.

"Well I got the story from Janice who lives in that apartment building round the corner, you know the girl with those four bad behind kids? Worse kids were never born, I'm telling you, and all of them got different fathers."

"You gonna' tell the story Ida or dog out them poor children?" Aunt Charlie interjected to cut off another story born out of the one she hadn't told yet.

"Well anyhow, the way I heard it, he came home and found the two of them all wrapped together like husk on corn."

I joined Kala on the steps to listen more closely to the gossiping women. In my mind, I could picture them nodding in unison to encourage the speaker to continue with her story. "The way I hear it, he tiptoed over to the bed, but they were so engaged they didn't even notice until he switched on the table lamp. His wife was wrapped up in the arms of some white woman she works with." A nervous giggle filled the room.

"That white woman started screaming like somebody was killing her."

"Well they say it can feel like that," Miss Sylvia added in her scratchy voice. "Been a long time since I felt that way though."

"Probably thought she was about to be killed," Miss Carol from across the street interjected.

"Anyways, he grabs her around the throat and pulls her right up to his face and starts kissing her on the lips."

"What?" they sang out in one choir note.

"Starts kissing her and strips off his clothes and climbs right in between them. Said there was no way they were leaving him out of it."

The room burst into laughter, Kala joining in with her mouth covered to muffle the sound.

"Now you know that's a lie," Aunt Charlie said.

"That's the way it was told to me," Miss Ida said. She never did like her gossip to be questioned. "Besides, you know how men are, Charlie." A silence as thick as the smell of burning hair filled the room, and I imagined that everyone found something on the floor to stare at.

"You're finished Ida," he replied with a snap of plastic. We figured that he must have snatched his smock from around her neck.

"Now don't go getting angry Charlie, I'm only speaking the truth." The chair scraped loudly and I knew she had gotten up to admire her hair in the wall mirror.

"Mind your business Ida," said Miss Carol. "Move on out my way now. It's my turn. I'm thinking I might want to try a short cut Miss Charlie."

"Me and Carol saw you arguing with that man up on the Avenue a couple of weeks ago," Miss Ida said. She couldn't let it go. "Looked like a lover's quarrel to us." The pungent smell of a newly lit cigarette floated up to our position on the steps.

"Ida get your behind out of here with that cigarette," said Aunt Charlie. "I'm thinking maybe you shouldn't come back next week. Go on up on the Avenue and let that Korean lady with the rotten fruit do your hair."

"Whew Miss Charlie, girl I didn't mean to upset you, I really didn't," she replied, panic filling her voice. She had gone too far and the whole room knew it. "I was just joking with you, that's all, just a joke."

What man? Kala mouthed. I shrugged my shoulders.

"My business is my own, don't nobody better forget that," Aunt Charlie declared. But his voice was shaky, almost as if he was afraid.

A few hours later, as I rode with him to West Philly to pick up his custom-made full-length winter coat, I asked one of my stupid questions. The red light had caught us at 40th and Parkside Avenue and he was busy fiddling with the buttons on the car radio.

"When did you know Aunt Charlie?"

"Know what, chile'?"

"That you liked to be with men and not women?"

His face sagged like I had just stuck a pin in his chiseled cheekbones and his fingers fell from the radio buttons like they had suddenly heated up beyond touching. I regretted the question before it fully left my mouth, but I couldn't take it back.

172

"I'm sorry Aunt Charlie," I whispered, wishing at that moment to be a contortionist so I could stick both of my feet in my big mouth.

"Don't worry about it," he said going back to twisting radio buttons, a big smile on this face and the red shadow of the traffic light falling on his smooth chocolate skin. Even in the dark that engulfed his small car, I could see him struggling with the answer to my question.

That night Kala's nightmares, the ones she started having that first month after my father died, returned. Horrible glimpses of her life before he died. Visions of blood mixed with a white gritty material all over her hands, feet and finally her face. They were smothering dreams that left her wet, shaking and screaming in the night.

"Kala girl, wake up." Aunt Charlie shook her gently, his eyes filled with concern and worry. "It's only a dream baby, only a dream."

Clutching his strong arms, desperate to escape the nightmare, she cried, "He's dead Aunt Charlie. Dead. I didn't want him to die, not to die, just to stop." She was hysterical. "Why wouldn't he stop?"

"Hush now baby girl. It's over," he said, rocking her gently. I sat up rubbing the sleep from my eyes. The stark whiteness of Aunt Charlie's satin pajama top bounced against the muted yellow of the hallway light bulb creating a Madonna and Child effect. He pulled Kala onto his lap and pressed her stocking cap covered head against his huge flat chest. I wanted to ask where his breasts went at night, but that time I did keep my mouth shut.

"What's going on?" I asked instead.

"Go on back to sleep, your sister had a bad dream, is all," Aunt Charlie whispered. "Everything is just fine now. Aunt Charlie is here. Aunt Charlie is here." And Kala began to cry even harder with that.

"Why did he do that Aunt Charlie? Why did they hate us?" My heart felt like it would burst as I watched him rock her just like she was a little ole' baby and not the teenage girl who had watched over us all these years. I realized then that she had never been a child, had never been held like that before, in the arms of someone who just wanted to love her. I couldn't hardly see, my eyes drowning in a sea of salt water.

"Shush now," he repeated over and over. "Hush now. I guess you're ready to hear it, so I guess I'm going to tell it – 'bout your momma, my sisters and my father." He waved me over then wrapped one of them big arms around my trembling shoulders and drew me tight. "Some things you just don't wanna' relive, but then comes the season, and the roots of a thing just grows right out of you anyhow." He took a deep breath, his chest rising and falling, and began.

"It was three of us, probably more at some point, but only two left by the time I came along – me, your momma and your Aunt Rachel." I opened my mouth to ask a question but he placed a finger on my lips to silence me. "Not yet little one, not yet,"

174

said Aunt Charlie. I laid my head against his chest and let the rhythm of his breathing satisfy me as he spoke. "Your momma was six years older than me and your Aunt Rachel was four years older than her, but there were four or five tiny little graves out in the back field." (I knew Kala had to be thinking about that little grave in the back of our house because I was.) "I asked about those graves once, but we never really spoke about it. Too busy trying to survive I guess. Anyway, The first thing I remember about my father is that he beat the shit out of my mother every chance he got, which was every day since he never went nowhere and neither did she. We worked for a white man name of Milner, James Milner and it was his farmland we worked. Your grandparents were sharecroppers and I like to think that they believed that one day they would work their way out of that dirt and own something. But they never did. In fact, every year we seemed to owe Mr. Milner more and more for the opportunity to work his land and the little bit of supplies he provided us with throughout the year."

"But why did y'all stay," I asked unable to contain the question.

He took a deep, sad breath before continuing.

"See honey that was how they kept us from ever leaving: Pay low wages and raise the prices on the supplies so your workers can't never get away – that how it was done. This made my daddy mad, real mad. It wasn't nothin' we did, it was just that he had us, and felt trapped by his own flesh. He was an angry man, angry and scared of Mr. Milner who he couldn't take his anger out on, so he took it out on the only folks around—us. When I was about 7 or 8 and your

momma was 13 or so, he got the idea that he could make enough money to get away from Mr. Milner by selling his daughters.

He started with you Aunt Rachel. Took her up to the local truck stop and worked her until she couldn't take it no more and drowned herself in the low stream behind Mr. Milner's house," he moaned. "She left a note for him that said, "I hope my death is at least worth a year's amount of groceries for y'all. It wasn't - day after a pine box funeral we were right back to work for the Milners."

I could feel myself suffocating for the Aunt I'd never met. Kala could too, by the sound of her breathing.

"Month after she died, we were sitting down to dinner when he came home with a pretty little pink dress for Ann, your momma. Had her try it on and strut up and down to show it off. He pulled her into a hug and said he was proud of her and that she was ready. Somebody had to replace Rachel and she was the only one left. My momma tried to stop him, held on so tight to Ann's little hand that one of her fingers almost bent backward. He beat her mother unconscious, left her lying in that stinking brown dirt, her soft hair blowing around her face. Laid there for so long I thought he'd kilt her. "

I pressed my ear harder against his chest, somewhat muting the hoarseness of his voice. The middle of night seeped like a black mist into the room as his warm, sour breath floated above our heads. It was the telling of a ghost story, my mother's story and felt as though it was somehow finally putting her to rest.

176

"Your momma was screaming and crying something awful and although she never had nothin' good to say or do for me, I started crying because I didn't want her to die like Rachel. I ran and got Miss Patina, who came and helped me carry momma into the house. But my father and Ann didn't come back until the middle of the night, him drunk as a skunk, and Ann, poor Ann, with a swollen lip and smelling of men and gasoline. She had an empty look in her eyes that reminded me of the well behind our house—black and hollow. My father took her 'bout every night after that and our momma tried to fight him, but each time he beat her down so bad. After a while she just couldn't fight him no more."

"So she was whore then, always been that," Kala said, pulling away from Aunt Charlie."

"Not always chile, just after he turned her out. Before that she was just a little girl making dolls out of paper," he answered, his voice filled with deep grief.

"Miss Patina, the lady who came by here to see you, she was my momma's best friend from childhood. She bought momma some money and told her to take it and get away. But that very same night, he took your momma, Ann, out again and we couldn't leave without her. She told me that we would be leaving in the morning, right after he left to go fix the fence Mr. Milner had been complaining about all week. And we did, we got away. We got to the main road on foot and Miss Patina was supposed to meet us there and drive us into town. But when we got there..." Aunt Charlie's voice lowered to a soft whisper and I could hear his heart pounding like a hammer. *"My father was waiting for us, had saw her car just sitting there idling and knew something wasn't right."*

"My momma said she was leaving, was taking her only two left and never coming back. My father hit her so hard that she fell, her head bounced off the steel bumper of Miss Patina's old Chevy, and split wide open like a dropped watermelon. Miss Patina jumped on him then, pounding her tiny fists into his back, but he threw her to the ground and told her to stay there or he would kill her. Then he picked up my momma and carried her like a bag of apples across his shoulder. He looked at me and Ann, and we knew if we didn't go back with him he was going to just let her die."

Aunt Charlie's heart was beating so fast, hard chest rising and falling so rapidly, that I had to sit up straight for a minute to get away from the terror I felt in his body. I wanted him to stop, thought the telling would kill him if he didn't, but he gripped us tighter and kept on talking.

"When we got back to that dirt shack he threw my momma on that old piece of bed she had slept on with him every night. Told Anna she better fix her up, "fix her up good 'cause if she died she would become his wife". Then he dragged me out to the yard and made me dig a hole, a big hole. It took me hours. I just kept digging 'cause he was standing there with his rake poking me like a bale of hay. Every time I tried to rest, I knew he was going to stab me so I just kept digging. The burning sun turned to cool rain, but I still continued digging. When he thought that hole was deep and wide enough, he told me to climb in and lay down. Piles of wet dirt and stones peppered my face, but I didn't care. I just didn't want to hurt no more. So I lay there, stiff like I was dead already, listening to that awful scraping sound that told me he was raising that old shovel again."

178

Aunt Charlie was crying and my grief for him bubbled up from the pit of my stomach like acid. *"Couldn't hear nothin' but silence," he continued. "I knew my momma lay dying inside on that filthy straw mattress and somehow that hurt me more than the struggle in my lungs as they fought for air. I knew I was going to die in that black hole and I was okay with that death."*

"But how did you get out Aunt Charlie?" Kala burst in. "How could you have survived that hole?"

"Believe or not, it was that white man, Mr. Milner, who saved me. He came looking for my daddy mad as a wet hen over his fence not being fixed. My father dropped the shovel so he could try to explain why it wasn't done—your momma told me that 'cause I was half-dead already and couldn't see or hear. At the same time Miss Patina and her husband came over to confront him about knocking her to the ground. She was the one who spotted my grave. Dropped to her knees and started digging me out with her bare hands. She saved me, and I was sorry for it at that moment," Aunt Charlie ended. "But that was a different season and out of that dirt my roots grew. After that day I wasn't scared of him no more. In fact I think he was a little scared of me. See, I was a walking ghost. I had died down there in that hole, but climbed out and brought life back with me."

Day was breaking through the cracks in our shade. He had talked nearly all night and there was still more we needed to know about him. I clutched the muscles in his arms so he wouldn't let me go, afraid this chance might not come again.

179

"Couple years later your daddy drove into the truck stop, and your momma didn't come back home. My father had stopped going with her by then. He knew she didn't think nothin' of herself and wasn't goin' nowhere. But he was wrong," Aunt Charlie said with a sad laugh. *"He was wrong about a lot—like when he thought his straight was gonna' to best a royal flush and he lost his piece of truck in a card game. He was wrong when he thought he could pull a knife on a man who carried a gun. And if he thought we would cry over his grave, he was sure wrong about that. A year later I lied about my age and joined the Marines. Was in there that I found out that I like the boys a whole lot better than the girls. For eight years, my jarhead brothers beat the hell out of me for my choice, but they never did realize that nothing could ever be worse than that hole back on Mr. Milner's farm."*

"When you were born Kala, my momma moved up here to see about you and we lost contact. When Ann called to tell me she was dead, I sent money to bury her but I just couldn't bring myself to come see her dead in a box."

"Why'd you come when I called?" Kala interrupted.

"Because I knew it was time for you to climb out of your hole, honey. You've been buried a long time. I can dig you out, but you gotta' take the breath necessary to step into your season. It's time honey, come into your season, Kala."

CHAPTER SIX - Love Jones

"*Silly of me to think* *that I could ever have you for my guy, how I love you"*, Charlie crooned behind his bedroom door. Aunt Charlie was in love. I didn't know why I didn't realize that before, but now his every movement told of the fact. Always meticulous about his appearance, he took extra time to put on his make-up and spent an hour rushing around his room deciding what to wear. He threw different colored, short and long wigs around the room and sang maddening love songs. It was times like these when I forgot Charlie was a man. In the six months he had lived with us he had been more of a mother than his sister ever was, but the fact that he cared deeply for someone else not only angered Kala, but it frightened her terribly. A lot had changed in the four months after our all-night conversation, all for the good. But Aunt Charlie's dating threw an unexpected monkey wrench into Kala's world. To say he favored her over the rest of us would be to minimize the intensity of their relationship. She worked harder at school than ever before and excelled because she wanted to please him. Long after we had been sent to bed the two remained downstairs, heads together in conversation.

So as Aunt Charlie descended from his bedroom, dressed in silver and white from head to toe, with flowing straight black hair and soft pastel lips, it was Kala's face I concentrated on. I saw her wince with jealously and roll her eyes. Clutching a new purse, Aunt Charlie swung around to model his outfit for us, a big smile spread wide across his face.

"Ooh, Aunt Charlie you're beautiful," I proclaimed.

Kala fumed under a pretense of watching something frustrating on television.

"When I get married I want to look just like you," added Sonny in a soft whispery voice.

"No you don't, stupid." The words slipped from between Kala's clenched teeth. Aunt Charlie rolled his eyes in her direction and ignored the remark.

"Well thank you, Mr. Sonny. That is surely a fine compliment."

"Me too!" Baby added, rubbing his hands carefully over Charlie's beaded dress.

"Good night children," Aunt Charlie said over his shoulder as he tiptoed out the front door taking care to protect the hem of his dress from the splintered edges at the bottom of the door. When Kala heard his car pull away, she ran into our room and angrily threw open one of her many textbooks to study. Aunt Charlie treated her special like and she didn't like it one bit that there was a part of his life that she wasn't privy to.

Guess I didn't care much about Aunt Charlie's love life because I was in love too, with Jeremiah Moore, one of the most popular boys in the sixth grade and an avid basketball player. He was my cooking partner in Home Economics, and I dreamed of the day when we could play house together for real. We spent hours on the telephone talking about everything and nothing, whispering childhood promises of family and togetherness.

Baby fell in love too, with a cat he named Simon (which none of us never did understand). The orange and white stray showed up on our front porch one rainy day in winter, just as Baby was being let off his special bus. Aunt Charlie opened the door to let him in, and he walked in with a huge smile on his face and Simon hidden under his raincoat. Nobody even knew he had the cat until dinner, when we felt raggedy fur scratching our ankles at the dinner table. "Rat," we yelled.

Aunt Charlie beat every last one of us up out of his chair, his famous lasagna forgotten for the moment. Then he charged the closet for the broom and the rest of us stood up in unison on our chairs, including Baby, who *knew* it was his stupid cat under the table. When we saw that it was a cat, Sonny threatened to blow up the darn thing. Kala was mad as a rabid dog and Aunt Charlie was laughing so hard that his curly brunette wig flew off his big head and hit the refrigerator. The kitchen went berserk as Simon raced back and forth underneath the table.

Finally, Baby jumped down from his chair and held his arms out for Simon who leapt into in his lap. "My cat," he said proudly as Simon purred.

"Where the hell did that cat come from?" Brother demanded.

"Watch your mouth boy!" Kala said, threatening him with a pretend swat as she climbed down off of her chair. "Baby, what're you doing with a cat?"

"My cat," he repeated as we went back to eating dinner now that the danger was over.

"Oh, no you don't," Kala commanded. "Put that thing outside, boy."

"No," he said stubbornly shaking his head. "No Kala, my cat. He's taking me to Heaven."

"What are you talking about boy?" she asked, reaching for the hissing cat who swiped at her with jagged claws.

"Alright, alright. Sit down and eat," Aunt Charlie said, pulling his wig over the stocking cap on his head. "We can talk about this after dinner."

But after dinner Baby still refused to let go of Simon and that settled the matter. I'm sure that if Kala, Aunt Charlie or any of us had any idea what pain Baby's love jones would cause, we would have tossed that beautiful cat back out in the rain. Thirteen days after Simon moved into our home, Baby was dead.

Stumbling from the Oasis, a neighborhood bar well known for loud music and watered-down liquor, a young couple witnessed the accident. They later explained how the pitch-black night had suddenly lit up like a Halloween fireworks show with a curtain of burning orange sparks shooting into the sky. Smoke rose from the ground and the air was filled with a metallic smell that they couldn't recognize. Holding hands, they fell to their knees drunkenly asking God to forgive them their sins. Their brains hazy and thick from low-shelf liquor, they thought it was the Second Coming of Christ. It was only later, after the police and ambulance had arrived, that they realized what had actually happened.

The trolley car couldn't stop. It pushed Baby for nearly two blocks, and when it finally came to a screeching halt, he and Simon were mangled beneath its front. It was bad, real bad. "Boy died instantly, him and the cat," the distraught trolley operator explained to the police as they walked him back and forth trying to piece the story together. "Wasn't nothin' for the rescue boys to save!"

We never knew for sure why Baby and Simon had gone outside in the middle of a gray chilly night, why they would be on the trolley tracks that Baby normally abhorred. That thought haunts us still to this day. But there are some things I will never forget from that night. The hammering on the front door, and the sense that something was very, very wrong the second I opened my eyes. The saliva crust whitening our lips as we stared in shock at the ghostly figure of Aunt Charlie's white winter robe flapping wildly in the freezing air. The heavy sound of his large feet as he raced toward the trolley car calling out - "Baby! Baby!" Blue uniforms holding us back so that we could only see the red, white and blue flashing lights atop their cars and only imagine what poor Baby must look like lying underneath the green and beige monster.

Kala threw her thin frame against the brawny bodies of the police officers crying "He's my baby! He's my baby!" until the strength simply slipped out of her legs and she fell to the sidewalk sobbing and broken - I thought beyond repair. I wrapped my arms about Sonny and Brother's shivering bodies, and said a silent prayer - me, the one who hated our trips to church. Tears gathered in the bottom of our eyes lids, but thicken before they could fall. Already we felt the link had been broken, Baby's soul had escaped the concrete that held it to this world.

Months later, I could still hear Kala's cries everywhere - in the soft crinkling of a balled-up TastyKake wrapper, the tin-based music of empty soda cans rolling along windy streets, in the colic whine of one of the Bakers' twin girls who lived around the corner, six doors down – always, surprising and painful.

CHAPTER SEVEN - Laying Down Your Burdens

It rained for four days after Baby's death, but the morning we chose to bury him, the sun sat so high in the sky that I had to shield my eyes in order to look upwards. As we climbed into the black limousine that would take us to Baby's funeral, everybody agreed that it was him smiling down on us one last time. Aunt Charlie sold his beautiful red car to pay for the funeral, the finest lay-your-people-to-rest outfits the Avenue had to offer, and a beat-up gray station wagon with two missing hubcaps. Although they said there wasn't much left of him, Baby would not be cremated or left on a SEPTA bus. No, he would have a real funeral, worthy not only of our love and respect, but also of our community's.

As we rode in silence through the streets of the concrete jungle, Aunt Charlie and Brother facing me, Kala and Sonny, the view through the tinted windows of the car felt dirty and cold. I was surprised by the quiet of our noisy block - the emptiness of Mrs. Smithfield's windowsill and the darkness of Mr.

Turner's barbershop. During the short ride to the funeral home, only the sound of sniffles and dry coughs disturbed the silence of the car. When the car stopped in front of the funeral home, and the driver opened the doors for us, no one moved. Finally Aunt Charlie said, "Let's go children," and swung his thick, stocking-covered legs out of the car. We followed him meekly, like little black lambs to the slaughter.

Sobbing, I stood in front of the funeral home blocking Sonny and Brother from leaving the car. Aunt Charlie had to come back and take my hand because my feet refused to move. Kala, Sonny and Brother patted me gently on the back.

Our entire neighborhood appeared be inside the funeral home, Miss Ida, her lip hanging low like she was smoking an invisible cigarette,. Mr. Turner in a burgundy polyester suit that looked like your hand would slide right off of it if you touched it. Mrs. Smithfield, who left her window two times in one year for funerals, and the white family from next door who borrowed more sugar than it bought. I nodded at Jeremiah (who winked sadly at me), and his parents, Mr. and Mrs. Rush.

We hurried past Mr. Henry, who had not been charged in our mother's death and still cried when he saw us. We also bypassed Mrs. Kelly, who was looking more skeletal than ever. Even Pinky, who wore his hair pulled back in a long ponytail and gold hoops in his ears, was there with sorrow lining his face.

The ushers from our church, dressed in white from head to toe, passed out fans with Jesus' face on the front and the slogan, "Jackson's Funeral Home: Bring your sorrows to Jackson's," on the back. Aunt Charlie, dressed in a black chiffon dress, with black netting covering his face, squeezed my hand as we approached the miniature white coffin that held Baby's broken body.

Behind me I could hear the hoarse crying of Brother and Sonny and the clicking of the half-size-too-large heels Aunt Charlie had purchased for Kala. Three feet away from Baby's coffin, as I was struggling to steady my wobbly knees, a man stepped out from the pews and reached for my hand. I didn't recognize him, clean-shaven, dressed in black and blue with gold tassels across his shoulders. I read the nametag attached to his chest as he offered a large smile, his eyes glistening with joy and pain. I screamed his name.

"NOODLE!"

We charged him unabashedly. Me, Sonny and Brother, gave and accepted hugs as we ignored stares from the funeral director, the pastor, the ushers, and Aunt Charlie, who looked thoroughly embarrassed by our behavior. Noodle was back, and suddenly that knowledge lightened the pain in our hearts just a little bit. He reached for Kala, but she ignored his hand and gripped one of Aunt Charlie's muscular arms. Together the two of them walked to Baby's closed coffin. We followed, hanging on to Noodle's arm.

"Wonder if he peed in that coffin," Brother said loudly, making everyone in the church crack up, including Aunt Charlie who almost doubled over. Kala was the only one who didn't laugh. She stared at us so coolly that we finally stopped. Only an hour and a half later—because Baby was just a sweet little boy and didn't have any outstanding sins or feats—the limo dropped us at our front door. The neighbors were already waiting with armloads of food, liquor and money.

"Thank you for coming," Aunt Charlie said, pulling off his pillbox hat as we entered the house. "Please come right on in." He gently pushed Kala, who was absentmindedly standing in the doorway, out of our guests' way.

"Yeah, come in," she muttered, opening the screen door with the missing screen wide for the parade of people.

Throughout the day so many people came through our house that we were beginning to feel like grinning puppets. Folding chairs were brought over from the church, but most guests chose to stand. Pastor Peifoy and most of the church members stayed in the living room with Kala and the boys, offering words of comfort and prayer.

The drinkers—this included about everybody else from the concrete jungle—quickly headed to the kitchen where Aunt Charlie was pouring bottles of corn liquor, gin and vodka into bowls of fruit punch. I kept finding excuses to go into the kitchen, staying longer and longer each time and receiving nastier looks from Kala upon each return to the living room. Poor Brother and Sonny were pinned firmly to the couch, next to Kala, who kept fussing with the collars of their white shirts and adjusting their black ties. Misery cratered their round faces. I was sure the pain I saw there was not only due to the loss of Baby, but to the pinching of their brand new shoes.

The only relief they had was when Sister Alvaline, the pastor's sister, ended up with the wrong cup of punch and her prayers turned into more giggles than godly words. By nightfall the "saved" folks left, asking us for the fourth or fifth time if we were going to be okay with "these old fools running around." They never said it, but it was clear that they despised Aunt Charlie and his friends. Kala finally convinced them that we would be fine and walked them to the front door.

We were officially free to attack the rows of fried and barbequed chicken, the potato salad, the collard greens, the sweet potato poon and the fresh baked biscuits smothered in salted butter. The cabinets were lined with all kinds of pies and cakes and a large bowl of Miss Ida's ambrosia that no one wanted to touch. Sonny made the mistake of going back into the kitchen for another chicken leg and Aunt Charlie forced him to take a bowl out of politeness. "But it tastes like a plate of spit!" he cried. We lost our appetite for "seconds" after that.

Noise filled our house as drunk people bathed us in their sloppy kisses, laughing about things that didn't involve Baby. I think we all felt the same, but I was the first one to put on my coat and slip out to the stoop. I think I knew Noodle would be waiting, which is why I headed outside instead up to the sanity of our bedroom. "Hey baby girl," Noodle said with a sweet, wide grin. "I was wondering how long it would be before you came to find me." I punched his arm in a teasing manner, my heart nearly exploding with the joy of seeing him.

"Why you just coming home," I asked. He looked so handsome in his blue Marines uniform that I wanted to cry. I think at that moment I realized that I had a little crush on Noodle.

"I've been around, watching from a distance," he answered, pulling me close. I buried my face in his dress jacket. He smelled freshly starched with a hint of Old Spice. "Missed you a lot though."

"Me too. Kala too. Sonny, Brother and Baby too," I said before remembering. A split second later I did, and it cut through me like a heated blade. "Well Baby missed you before he died."

"Baby was a good boy. But you know what happened wasn't nobody's fault, right?" Noodle asked.

"I think Kala blames herself."

"Of course she does. He was her baby."

Noodle and I stood, side by side, him much taller and stronger than I would ever be. "You her baby too, you know?"

"Why is she treating you so mean?" I asked, already knowing the answer but wanting to see if he did.

"Look at those lights down there," Noodle said, pointing southward toward the tall buildings of Center City. "Let me tell you, I've seen things that make those buildings pale in comparison. Remember when we thought that was all we could have?" I nodded, confused by this Noodle. "The day before I was getting out of jail, a Marine recruiter came to speak to the guys who'd only done short time. They said instead of coming back to the same streets and situations that

191

landed us there, that we could come with him tomorrow, join the Marines. It was an opportunity to change our lives."

"And you went?" I asked, dumbfounded by his daring and courage, as I turned to stare at the twin 18-story buildings in the middle of the concrete jungle. It was really the first time I had seriously thought that leaving was possible.

"Baby girl, I don't know how I decided. But before I knew it, I had signed the papers and climbed into the van they had waiting outside. Only one other guy joined me, and we were flanked by four of the biggest dudes we'd ever seen." Noodle laughed lightly, his baritone voice filling the crisp evening air. "We landed in San Diego, California, and I thought I'd died and gone to heaven. There are palm trees there and the bluest water in the biggest seas you've ever seen. At first we were stumbling around like two bumpkins, thinking it was sort of a vacation, but reality set in quick enough. They threw some uniforms on us then put us in a group of about 25 other guys, and next thing we knew we were marching through woods, along beaches, sometimes buck-naked except for our boots in 100-degree weather. They thought they were going break us, going to kill us, and they tried with their basic training. But deep down inside, we were tougher."

"But why didn't you tell us? Why didn't you come home?"

"I could have come home; I wanted to. I was missing my brothers, sisters, you and Kala so bad that I went off and hid in the crapper so I could cry without anybody seeing me," he said in a voice that made me believe him. Again he pulled me toward him. "Don't you see? Coming home, coming back to this jungle could have made me turn cold again inside. I feel warm now, baby girl, warm and alive without all this concrete holding me in. I have to make some honest money so I can take care of my sisters and brothers. I have to get them out. Ain't that what Kala's been doing for y'all for the last couple of years?"

"Where are they, your brothers and sisters?" I wasn't going to tell him that his little sister Sassy had been spotted hanging with the local drug dealers and was reputed to be heavy in the drug game herself.

"I got everybody settled except Sassy," he said proudly. My eyes fell to his black spit shined boots. "I already know about Sassy. I still got a lot of people out on these streets. I don't know how I'm going to help her just yet, still working on helping the other ones." I followed his eyes through the living room window until they landed on Kala who appeared to be interested in a conversation Mr. Turner was having with the room full of people. "I got my C.O. to write a letter to the welfare people telling them I was in the service, and had already been promoted to Sergeant. I'm doing good, you know. We convinced them to let the kids go live with my mother's sister in Georgia. She only has one son and she's willing to take them along with the checks she'll get from the welfare department in Georgia and the ones I'll be sending her from my military pay." He smiled and his face appeared to light up like a round Christmas bulb. "She has big house on some land their daddy left them when he died. Ain't a drop of cement nowhere. Good schools and plenty to eat."

"They won't ever come back?" I asked, shocked. Inside I could hear the repast finally winding down, and Kala yelling at Brother about something or the other. Maybe he had finally gotten into the Boones Farm wine like he'd been promising to do all evening long.

"For what, baby girl?" he asked then pointed up at the stars in the sky. "See those there? They look the same all over the world. You can take them with you—you don't have to stay here on this stoop. That's what I came back to tell you."

And suddenly, for no particular reason, I knew he was right. "Baby didn't make it out, but you can. All of you can."

Noodle waited in the cold for Kala, easily like it was nothing for over an hour. Then he left. By that time everybody had been gently shoved out the door and Aunt Charlie and Miss Kelly (the lady with the eating problem), were quietly straightening up. I reached for the broom to join them, but he waved me up the stairs. His eyes were as red as the fruit punch they'd been drinking all night. I tiptoed into our bedroom but I could tell that Kala was still awake. I climbed in the bed thinking over Noodle's words. As I drifted off to sleep I thought I heard crying in Sonny and Brother's room, but I was just too tired to investigate the whimpering. There would be a lot more tears in the days to come - I was sure of it.

The tears and the pain weren't long in coming. We had missed four days of school and had to return the next morning. I was secretly relieved. The spirits in

194

our house felt too heavy to carry around anymore and I wanted to escape the sorrow. Kala insisted on blaming herself although there was no way she could have known that Baby would wander out into the street and get hit by the #23 trolley in the middle of the night. In a week's time, she had dropped so much weight that Aunt Charlie was angrily concerned. That's the way it was with Aunt Charlie. If he was worried, it made him angry that he had to be worried. He preferred life as laid back and simple as possible.

We came home after that first day of returning to school to discover that Aunt Charlie had made each one of us our favorite meal. Spaghetti and meatballs for me; fried chicken and macaroni and cheese for Sonny; salmon cakes and rice for Brother, and, for Kala, fried flounder, grits and gravy. We all shared a sweet potato pie topped with whipped cream for dessert. The house smelled spicy and sweet, of hot sauces and vanilla, burning hair and perm cream since customers had come and gone all day while he prepared the feast. We rushed to finish our homework, then everybody but Kala, who almost had to be dragged down to the table, ran to eat. Once she took her seat, she stared intently at Baby's empty chair.

It wasn't long before Aunt Charlie started slamming plates and silverware around and mumbling about "people not appreciating what people do for them." Without a doubt the tension that had been brewing since the death of Baby was about to erupt. Sonny, Brother, and I didn't want any part of it. We ate as quickly as possible and had just thanked Aunt

Charlie for our slices of sweet potato pie when Kala finally reached a boiling point.

"You think it's *my* fault don't you?" Kala asked of no one in particular, her face pointed down toward her still-full plate of food. "I didn't mean to let him die!"

"I don't think that at all," I said quickly.

"Me neither," piped in the boys at the exact same time, which was strange because that never happened.

"I should have watched him closer, made him sleep with me."

"You mean us?" I asked, dumbfounded. "You wanted Baby to pee on *us* every night?"

"But you're a pee pot yourself," Brother said in his squirrely changing voice. "Every time we turn around, you're peeing your pants."

"Shut up! That was a long time ago," I screamed although, I had only just stopped peeing on myself in the last three months or so. Aunt Charlie said I'd stopped worrying so much, had less to carry around in my bladder. Sometimes I hated Brother.

"Stop it you two!" Aunt Charlie ordered before turning to the sobbing Kala. "Okay girl, it's time to lay your burdens down." (I love Aunt Charlie's little quirky sayings.) "Cause I'm telling you, that pain you're carrying is too heavy of a load."

"I sho—shoul—should have watched him b—b—better" Kala said between sobs. "He was my little boy and I let him down."

Brother and Sonny stood up to leave, but Aunt Charlie waved them back down. "My dream told me this was going to happen, I just didn't know who. I didn't know it would hurt this bad."

"Would it have hurt any less if it was Sonny or Brother or Baby Girl who's over there waiting for your answer?" Aunt Charlie asked gently. "Girl you ain't God and you don't control life and death."

"There was only four fish in the concrete pond, Aunt Charlie. Four fish! But I didn't want to see that part." She buried her face in her hands and we watched helplessly as tears squeezed through the cracks of her fingers and fell onto her half-eaten plate of food.

"Kala, I drove a couple hundred miles thinking of four fish. You're not the only one who has dreams honey," he said, folding his hands over his belly. "I had a pretty good business down South. I had my own hair salon and more than enough customers to keep me busy for years to come. But three days after you called about Ann, I had a dream when I hadn't had 'em for years."

He had our attention now. Sonny leaned in with his elbows on the table, and Brother's eyes were huge awaiting his next words. Kala dropped her hands and stared at him looked totally surprised and taken aback, as I nodded my head like he was a preacher giving his best sermon.

"In the dream I was standing by this small lake with a fishing pole, which was damn strange for me since I've never been a fisherman. But I'm standing on the edge of this lake and I see these fish struggling to get out, like they're trapped in that water and just can't stand to be in no more. I throw out my pole, and one after the other, I catch four beautiful black fish. Only thing is I know right away is that they're special, not for eating or throwing back. I know I'm supposed to save them."

He finished in a thick, husky voice.

"When I opened my eyes, I knew you kids were the ones in my dreams and I was supposed to come up here and see about you," his said, his voice cracking now. "But when I got here and saw five—five—kids, I knew what we all know now."

"Aunt Charlie you owned a hair salon?" Brother asked. The rest of us gave him a cold look, even Sonny, who normally ignored Brother's just plain stupid questions.

Aunt Charlie disregarded Brother's interruption and continued.

"So if it was anybody's fault that our beautiful little Baby was going to die, it was mine. I should've watched all of y'all a little bit closer." Teardrops mingled with his perfectly applied eyeliner, blackening his damp brown eyes. "Wasn't nothin' we could do to save Baby and if you dig down in yourself you'll know that's the God's honest truth!"

Almost instantly, the pain that had cratered Kala's face since the "accident" fell away – just dropped to the floor like an un-needed veil. With a look of relief and love on her face, Kala attempted to wrap her arms around Aunt Charlie's shoulders, but they didn't quite close.

"Sometimes you just gotta' lay down your burdens chile', 'cause they are just too heavy to bear."

"How many times are you going to rescue me Aunt Charlie?" Kala sobbed, with a wide smile this time.

"As many times as you need saving Kala – that's how many times."

About an hour later I opened our bedroom window to the shivering cold, and listened as Kala and Noodle talked about their hopes and dreams. I was happy that he had come back and that she had let him. Now they sat on the stoop laughing and holding hands, never noticing me peering down at them from the second floor. Kala asked about his sisters and brothers and Noodle told her of his plans to send them down south to his aunt. He had been to see every one of them and they were happy and excited that they would be together again.

"Found Sassy with one of the Ministers a few blocks over. She refused to come with me and it would have cost some blood for me to make her," he said, his deep voice rising. "I have to give the other kids a chance. That's what my mother would've wanted."

"I miss her Noodle," Kala inserted softly.

"Hurts me so bad - my mom not being here, but I'm going to make her proud, if I have to die doing it."

"No Noodle, please don't say that," said an alarmed Kala. "You can't die!"

"Of course I won't," he replied with a laugh. "Will you wait for me?"

"I don't know," Kala teased. "Will you come back Reynolds?"

"Girl, I told you not to call me that."

"Well you shouldn't have worn your name tag Sergeant Reynolds Mickins." I could tell she was proud that he had gone into the Marines, even if it meant they would be separated. "You're going to be gone a long time."

"Not long enough for you to drive me away Kala," he replied in a husky voice. "We are getting out of here together."

"Do you think we can Noodle? Do you really think we can?"

The sound of his laughter, rich and thick like that Alaga syrup on Miss Mickins butter filled biscuits filled the evening air, and I stretched my neck farther out of the window trying not to miss a word. "I'm already out Kala and you will be out soon. Just hold on to my words. Hold on to your dreams, tight as you can."

The #23 drove past slowly, as it had been doing since Baby was killed. Kala's response was blown away by the screeching metal and the clang of the trolley's signal bell. After about a minute the two red brake lights of the iron horse disappeared without incident toward Center City and I realized that I had been holding my breath. Across the street I could see Mr. Turner in the apartment over his barbershop cooking some dinner. I caught a glimpse of a female arm but couldn't quite make it out through the lace curtains in his kitchen window. The voice of Mr. Chuck, the new black husband of the white lady next door, drifted out the window. I chuckled, listening to him yell at her about her inability to "make a decent pot of red beans and rice."

In the distance I could hear what sounded like a baby crying, but knew it was probably Miss Ida's whoring cat Calico getting on with the big gray that had been wandering the neighborhood. Darn cat followed her everywhere, including our back door and Aunt Charlie had threatened to shoot the "nasty mongrel" if he showed up again. A new corner store had opened a block away and I could see its owner, Mr. Nicky, struggling to pull down the steel security gates that would keep his inventory safe for yet another night.

"...my prom?" Apparently I had drifted off and missed part of Kala's and Noodle's conversation. I stretched my neck trying to catch up.

"Kala, I'm promising you that I will be back to take you on your prom, so don't you ask any other guy to go with you, okay?" He was on his feet and looking so handsome in his uniform that my heart burst with pride. "Promise me Kala," he pleaded.

"I promise Noodle," she said sincerely, "as long as you come in full military dress."

They laughed easily together and he held out his hand to her. I stuck my head back in the window to give them some privacy. Noodle would be leaving in the morning. So much had changed in the last three years and as I stretched out across our shared bed, I smiled thinking of our lives and the future we were blazing towards.

CHAPTER EIGHT – The Happy Ending

I hate to use the clichéd "Happy Ending" here. I mean no one rode off into the sunset on a pure white horse, pausing for a moment to look back at their invisible audience with a satisfied smile. But the years did go by more peacefully and without another tragedy. The concrete jungle around us grew less inhibiting and less frightening as we stretched toward a future outside of its brick walls. In time and in stages, we all recovered from Baby's death. Eventually the moment came when we shared a laugh together about all of his loving antics and his beautiful smiles.

Two major things involving Aunt Charlie happened the spring after Baby's death. Some fellow by the name of Jheri Redding invented the Jheri Curl, a style that invaded African American communities all over the country and became all the rage in the concrete jungle. The Jheri Curl was a glossy, loosely curled look worn by Michael Jackson in the early part of the '80s, which of course made it a must for the young and old. Entire families turned curly haired over-night and I watched with envy as I sat under the straightening comb every Sunday night. Aunt Charlie hated the Jheri Curl, said it was "a sin and shame to walk around with your hair dripping juices all over the place", but never the fool he became a Jheri Curl expert for his clients. Power fist picks with steel teeth and spray holders for curl activator flew off the hair care shelves and every couch in the jungle had towels lined up on the headrests to protect them from excess juices. Aunt Charlie made so much money on the Jheri Curl that he eventually went into partnership with Mr. Turner and moved his business across the street into his barbershop.

I was angry with Aunt Charlie for refusing to give me one of his famed Jheri Curl's, but Michael Jackson's hair did catch fire the following January while he was shooting a commercial, which made me realize that he was probably right.

That spring, Aunt Charlie also hit 1462 on the street number for $5,000 and purchased all new furniture for the house, including new bedroom sets for everyone. Kala moved across the hall into our grandmother's old room (where she could watch over the grave of her dead baby), the boys got new matching twin beds, and I got a room all to myself. Since Kala and I had never been separated before, our split came with tears of joy and fear. Eventually we adjusted and grew to love our privacy.

That summer, the trolley car people showed up with a check for $25,000, although they still admitted no culpability in Baby's death. We took it as a miracle from God and Aunt Charlie deposited all of it in the bank for our college educations. Knowing that it was there waiting for us, we took our classes more seriously when school started in the fall, which greatly pleased both Kala and Aunt Charlie. In the 8th grade I decided that I would be a writer and Kala presented me with my first journal, which I filled up within a week.

Earlier that year the moonwalk was the biggest new dance in the jungle. Then in September, Vanessa Williams was crowned as the first Black Miss America and I spent hours practicing in the mirror with a tiara I made out of glue and aluminum foil. After watching me, Aunt Charlie encouraged me to join the modern dance team at school. By the end of the school year, my awkwardness had worn off and I had a body that both boys and men would whisper about when I walked past. "Filthy leeches!" Aunt Charlie would call out as they passed our front step a little slower than necessary.

Noodle wrote every week and Kala nearly knocked us down getting to the mail. I saw a peace in her, and the reddish-yellow pain that circled her beautiful brown irises grew smaller and smaller each year. On October 23, 1983 the United States Embassy in Beirut, Lebanon, was bombed killing 299 people. This didn't particularly impact our lives, but a few days later when Noodle called to announce that he was being sent to Grenada (to participate in Operation Urgent

Fury), a small island in the Caribbean Islands, we became extremely interested in world affairs. Later we laughed about how that war lasted only a few days and had fewer casualties than a gang war between the Ministers and the Diamond Street Rattlers.

Cocaine, previously the "white man's drug," ravaged the concrete jungle in the form of crack. Friends and neighbors turned into black ghosts floating all night throughout the neighborhood in search of their next hit. Aunt Charlie said it was the saddest thing he'd ever seen in his life. I started to tell him that we'd lived through sadder, but I didn't want to hurt him by bringing up the way my mother had lived.

That November, Brother announced that Sassy Mickins was "selling her behind" on the fire exit stairs of Building Number Two for $5 or a rock of crack. Kala and Aunt Charlie marched around there to get her but she refused to leave, which broke all of our hearts. In her next letter to Noodle Kala told him that Sassy was in trouble, but didn't go into the specific details.

The Jungle was changing. The sense of oneness we'd all shared, even in the middle of disputes and tragedy, was shattered as neighbors woke up to find the sons and daughters of friends, or the friends themselves, robbing their homes. Street wars evolved into drive-by shootings and Miss Ida was shot in the fatty part of her thigh as she made her way back home from a hair appointment at Charlie's and Turner's Hair Emporium (we still laugh about the name). Rumors spread through the jungle that it took the emergency room doctors an hour to find the bullet buried beneath the fat in her leg, and then they had to drain off a pound of fried chicken grease just to grip it with their instruments. Kala said that it was a lie, but Aunt Charlie winked at me and smiled.

The year Kala graduated from high school, Sonny became a Space Shuttle nut and spent the entire day watching the Discovery liftoff on television. Brother, still up to his antics (though they were less harmful), was caught spray-painting the walls of his junior high school. When the police brought him home, Aunt Charlie threatened to "whip his little behind," but no one took that seriously. His heart was too soft to ever go through with the threat.

"Well at least he didn't try to burn the place down," Kala commented after he'd been banished to his room for the next two weeks.

A month before her graduation, and a week after Noodle flew home to take Kala on her prom, an entire West Philadelphia neighborhood did burn to the ground in the MOVE incident Like the rest of the city we watched every detail on television, Brother safely in between Aunt Charlie and Kala on our living room couch. The members of the MOVE organization wore their hair in dreadlocks (which Aunt Charlie said was enough to make a man crazy), lived a naturalistic lifestyle and preached against technology. After a number of reports of waste materials in their house, and loud profanity-filled protests, the police attempted to remove the group from the neighborhood. The situation ended in tragedy when Mayor Goode—our first Black mayor—authorized bombing the house. His fire commissioner let the resulting fire burn, leading to the death of 11 MOVE members—including children—

and the destruction of the entire neighborhood of row houses. The incident left the entire city on edge, and for months I couldn't stand to hear the sound of a helicopter or airplane overhead.

On the morning of Kala's graduation, I woke up hungry. The feeling reminded me of a time that seemed like a lifetime ago but was actually a little less than five years ago. For a moment I lay there, still and silent, as if even my breathing would disturb that first quiet moment of the day that holds the rest in a tiny peaceful bubble. In that moment, the smell of frying fish, boiling grits and freedom exploded in my brain. A surge of pride crowded out all of my doubts and worries about our future. I got up, going to find Kala.

In her bedroom, I watched as she pressed her pink dress for a second time, the scent of a celebration breakfast filling the air. I decided right then that this moment was wholly related to Kala's determination to save us from our environment, and the sudden appearance of Aunt Charlie in our life. Kala would be the first of us to graduate high school, but not the last, according to Aunt Charlie. Memories of our father and my mother (Kala still refuses to take ownership) were waning, and we continued to flourish amidst the harshness of the concrete jungle.

"You smell that?" I asked.

She leaned back, her hand pressing down on the iron as steam rose up and moistened her face. "Smells like freedom to me," she replied, a knowing smile on her small lips. She unplugged the iron and laid her dress across her bed.

At the end of a day of caps, gowns and the most boring speeches of my life, we threw a huge party for the neighborhood that ended when Mrs. Brown from two streets over came looking for Mr. Brown who happened to be slow dancing with Miss Lois who lived on the 8th floor of the high rise. Pinky and his mother came, and he asked for my phone number, which made me sick to my stomach. Miss Ida gave Kala a crisp $50 bill with tears in her eyes. Kala said she was crying because she had already sealed the money in her graduation card and couldn't figure out how to get it back out without disturbing the envelope. The white lady from next door baked a lemon cake even though we still couldn't pronounce her name and Mr. Turner kept saying over and over again, "I knew you'd be something. I knew you'd be something." Sonny made her promise to send copies of all of her science homework because he wanted to get a head start, and Brother promised to stay out of trouble and not get arrested again. Aunt Charlie cried so much that his make-up turned into two brown streams, and I told him I would have to move my seat if he didn't stop.

The party ended with the kind of fireworks that made Aunt Charlie act more like Uncle Charlie, which we all found hilarious. As he hummed his favorite spiritual, collected pieces of wrapping paper, and sipped Boones Farm wine from a Styrofoam cup, we slipped out the front door and sat on the stoop.

Kala would leave for college in two weeks and this could very well be our last evening to share the spring moon, just the two of us. Warmth was just descending upon the city and a few kids were scattered throughout the long city block, getting an early start on summer vacation. The boys had been asleep for an hour, run up the stairs by Aunt Charlie toward the end of the party when Brother sipped out of a cup that he was supposed to be taking to the trash can.

"We're going to be okay," I said softly, waving away the moth that had been circling the dim porch light.

"I know," she replied wrapping her arm tight around mine. "Charlie loves you and the boys. He'll do right by us."

"He loves you most," I said, as she nodded and smiled. I was happy that she was special to Aunt Charlie, that she had someone to look out for her, protect her, and keep her safe.

"Nice to be lo—loved," she mumbled sleepily. I didn't answer. She'd stuttered on the last word and I felt her stiffen before she spoke again. "He's not like them."

"I know," I replied. "I know."

"I'm only a phone call away," Kala assured me, turning to grip my hands in hers.

"But I'm never gonna' call," I answered truthfully.

She had given up everything for us. This was her time, and I was determined that she would have it. "You have a chance. What do you plan to do with it?"

Her eyes lit up with that question, the first star of the night catching her iris at that very second. "Oh honey, it's a big world outside this concrete jungle. I think I'll just grab a pole and do a little bit of fishing."

The End

Coming Soon

From

Tina Smith-Brown

Brother

CHAPTER ONE - Change is Gonna Come

I woke up evil. Smell of Raid and frying bacon competing for my attention, I wiped my forehead, damp from sweat and leftover nightmares, with the back of my hand. Bad images, a lot of them, but I struggled to hold on to their shadows just a little bit longer. Sometimes my nightmares weren't as bad as my real life. My long, skinny legs curled automatically toward the growl roaring in the pit of my stomach – one of those real life moments trying to take hold.

A light breeze slightly raised my thin bedroom curtains and cowboys and Indians - one shooting, the other one running – rushed toward me. Good and bad decorated the ugly blue curtain, which hung crookedly from a cheap brass rod bent a long time ago. Through the thin walls I could hear bathtub water emptying with a thirsty gulp and my older sister Kelly ruining a song I couldn't exactly catch the words to. It was enough to force my eyelids open wide. She wouldn't leave a ring in the tub, like my brother. I loved her for that, in addition to a thousand other small things.

The toilet with the broken handle that you had to jiggle three times exact, ran freely, filling my head with the sound of running water. It was a school day. I sat up surrounded by blue. The color had been a gift from Aunt Charlie who'd painted our room a few months ago. I still hadn't grown use to the shade, which seemed to highlight the cracks in the walls that the dark brown paint had hidden.

"You two need some uplifting," he'd said, paint brush in one hand, roller in the other. "Waking up to blue makes everything alright."

I thought that he was wrong, but it made Aunt Charlie happy to do little surprises for us, so who was I to spoil his fun.

I would have rather black walls, with a million stars painted on the ceiling, but nobody had asked my opinion. Nobody asked me much about nothing, like they couldn't see me or somethin'. Most days invisibility worked in my favor, brought me less trouble - most days.

Aunt Charlie's thick voice cussing up a storm floated up like a warm bedtime story from the kitchen and I imagined the straw broom lifted high above his head as he chased a rodent of some kind out of his sanctuary. Aunt Charlie loved to cook, but he never could sit still for rodents, which made living in the concrete jungle a pretty miserable existence in my opinion. It was easier just to grow use. Grow use to the noise, the smell, and grow use to the rodents, both the four and two legged ones. Just grow use and survive until you escape, which most didn't think was possible. But I did. Kala did, had done.

The growl in my stomach grew louder which always made me think of our oldest sister Kala and the hunger and pain that only she could make disappear with words. And there had been a lot of hungry nights. Nights when she'd climb into our bed and sustained us with her warmth and dreams until each of us drifted off with a mind full of imagination, if not food.

Absentmindedly my hardened boy fingers curled into a fist at the memory of twirling them the same way about her two thick plaits. I'd asked her the same question over and over again struggling to understand the answer with my 3-year-old mind.

"But why can't we just go to the store and buy some food?"

Sometimes it hurt me real bad not having her arms around me every day, but Kala wouldn't be home for summer break for at least another month. I sat up slowly answering the call in my belly. Everything had changed in the last two years, the best thing being that we didn't have to worry about food any longer. We suffered hunger pains now only because we were too lazy to walk to Aunt Charlie's kitchen. The kitchen had been Aunt Charlie's since the day he arrived four years ago with a huge smile to match his huge hands. The breakfast he'd cooked that first morning after his arrival still lingered like a smile in the back of my mind. But I still hadn't grown used to eating breakfast to the smell of his expensive perfumes and the Pine sol he scrubbed the floor down with every night.

The #23 trolley whizzed by, gigantic steel wheels slightly shaking the floor beneath my feet. It made me think of Baby's crooked smile. "He's walking with Jesus now boy," is what Charlie said anytime I brought him up. That was his way of avoiding the hurt that I read on his face when he stared out the window at the empty trolley tracks. I think those were the moments he allowed himself to think of Baby, the night he died under the wheels of the trolley car. We all had our remembering Baby moments.

214

Like right then, as I rubbed my hands across the front of my boxer shorts, I leaned into my memory of Baby wetting our bed, the sad look on his face when I punched him hard in the arm. I'd bought him an orange Popsicle so that he wouldn't tell Kala. My sadness about Baby normally came like this, early in the morning, left over, like dew from the night before

My hated curtains felt clammy in my hands as I pulled them wide to allow sun and dampness to slip inside. The sidewalks were wet and a steel trashcan lay on its side on the cracked cement curb, fat drops of water ran slowly down its dented side.

Must have rained over-night, I thought. "And this place still stinks."

I spotted Mr. Turner, the "bloody barber" as we kids nicknamed him, struggling with a broken second floor window screen. It fell out of his wrinkled hands just missing Miss Ida's hair that looked like she'd slept without a scarf on overnight. I figured that she was headed towards the greasy spoon a few blocks up. She and Aunt Charlie had a falling out the week before so Miss Ida would have to pay for her breakfast until they repaired the damage. I pressed my elbows flat, like dead flowers, against the windowsill and braced myself for what was sure to come. Miss Ida never disappointed. I expected her to give Mr. Turner a verbal haircut like he'd never experienced before. But a second passing trolley car cut off my view and I missed the early morning sidewalk show. That made me want to cuss, but I knew Aunt Charlie would wash my mouth out with soap if he heard me. Sometimes Aunt Charlie could slip up the stairs soundlessly, which was when he was his most dangerous. After a few seconds Mr. Turner's baldhead disappeared inside the window, one of his dark brown, wrinkled hands waving an apology.

Still feeling evil, I didn't laugh at the hilarity of the scene, although as the #23 passed, I heard the hard laughter of several of our neighbors. A voice that sound like Eddie Young, the boy born with one ear call out, "Nat Turner those flies gonna eat cha' up if Miss Ida don't get to you first!" I almost smiled at that.

From a neighbor's bedroom window Stevie Wonder's "Living for the City" competed with the bawling of Miss Gemini's daughter Carissa's baby who lived three doors over in Miss Daisy Smithfield's old house. Miss Smithfield had only been dead from cancer three days when the projects people had moved them into her empty house.

Miss Gemini, a middle age "fox", was what the older folks called a "reader". They disappeared into her house only to come out again about fifteen minutes later carrying a large candle with a picture of "white" Jesus on the side. Miss Gemini and Carissa had six months in the concrete jungle (Fairhill Projects) and they appeared to be settling in for the long haul. The long haul was anybody who stayed over 10 years. Since I'd been born here, I was considered a lifer.

Miss Daisy Smithfield, who'd spent most of her day hanging out her bedroom window (hot or cold weather), died on New Year's Eve, an hour after she'd yelled for Brother to run to the store to get her a Stanback and bottle of ginger ale. He'd thrown a snowball at her window instead, and told "the old bat to go get it herself." That was the first time Aunt Charlie had ever hit one of us – slapped Brother clean across what he called his "lying lips" - when Miss Ida, who noticed that Miss Daisy was dead, had reported on what he'd done, and he'd denied it.

"Died with a frozen stare on her face, hands gripping the window sill," Miss Ida told Aunt Charlie. "Heart attack I think."

It took the police an hour and half to come and another two to get a wagon out since it was New Year's Eve and they expected a lot of murders. As they carried her body out of her house at 12:04 a.m., the New Year's sky lit up with the sounds of gunfire and drunken shouts of celebration. Mr. Turner and Miss Ida took a swig from the bottle Aunt Charlie (who'd had to cancel his New Year's Eve's plans) passed to them from the inner pocket of his winter coat. Each of them said something nice about Miss Smithfield, though in life couldn't none of them stand her. I waited for them to pour some out onto her step like in Cooley High, but they didn't. I guessed their friendship didn't extend into the eternity.

Change had been hard on the concrete jungle even if we didn't have thousand-year-old trees to cut away or wild animals to leave homeless. The invasion of our bricks had been just as devastating to the community. Everyone says I think too hard about these kinds of things, but I think they don't think enough about them. For those people, their world doesn't stretch further than the top of the eighteen story twin buildings of the projects, but mine, it goes all the way to the moon.

217

Mr. Turner and Miss Ida were two of the things in the jungle that would never change – I knew that for sure – and for some reason that little piece of knowledge gave me a sense of assurance. I had grown accustomed to her hard laughter and his dry wit. Rumor was that they had dated a few years back and that he had broken her heart. Kelly, the forever optimistic, announced one evening at dinner that they would find love again, to which Aunt Charlie gave a rare grunt and waved one of his perfectly manicured hands. They were Aunt Charlie's best friends in a neighborhood that shunned him for his homosexuality and his love of wearing women's clothes.

A block up, the steel gate that fell promptly at 9 P.M. each night over the front door of Nicky's grocery store with the number house in the back, rose with a loud screech. Within twenty minutes there would a line to the corner as people dropped off their number slips on the way to work. Since Miss Ida and Mr. Turner had "all day" they would walk down together at about 10 A.M. Every Friday morning Aunt Charlie pushed a dollar in my hand to play triple twos on the way to school 'cause Nicky didn't like Aunt Charlie much.

Most people in the concrete jungle didn't like Aunt Charlie. The women tolerated him because he was best hairdresser "on this side of the east coast", and the men left him alone because of his military background. But the teenage boys, they were stupid, stupid and mean. They hated Charlie because he was different and "teenagers can't stand nothin' different", he told me once after a fight at school. They hated us too, because we were his blood. But their fear of

Brother was more powerful than their hate for Aunt Charlie.

I got pretty good at ignoring the jonsing, and Brother's threats kept the fights to a minimum, but I felt like a fish in a boiling pot, my fins folding under the heat. It wasn't that I wanted him to leave us - it was just hard belonging to him while living in the projects. In the hood everybody had to belong to somebody.

"Oh that's Ada's boy."

"Hey, ain't Crystal your momma?"

"I'm gonna tell your daddy, Charlie Watson, from up on the fourteenth floor."

It was all we had and if you didn't belong to somebody you wasn't anybody. But still, it was hard belonging to Aunt Charlie, his strong male arms coated in soft, loving scents. It made me want to cry, how I felt about him – love and a little bit of hate too, at the same time. Kelly said he was, "way better than what we had before." She and Kala would know because they remembered a lot more about our parents. What I remembered, I wanted to forget.

The husband of the white woman who lived next door with her six kids was home for the moment tho' he came and went like the "mailman", according to Aunt Charlie. I eased dropped as he accused her of going into his wallet while he slept. It was joke 'cause everybody knew that he didn't have any money, was living off of her welfare check and food stamps, along with her kids. *"Kids, get in here and say goodbye to your momma, 'cause I'm about to kill her."* Too warm to shut my window I retreated from their war play, evil still riding my back like filth on a hog. Kelly said being around Aunt Charlie had us thinking and talking in a southern accent and I was starting to agree.

Tacked to the wall closest to the door hung a calendar from the China Palace Chinese/American restaurant. Half the days of the week of June were shaded by a large soy sauce stain, but I could see the large red circle around the date. June 19th - Juneteenth, my Black History teacher would tease me later that day at school. *"It's a very special day Sonny, and on your thirteenth birthday."* I placed my middle finger on the circled date and closed my eyes thinking of birthdays that had never been.

Behind me I heard my brother, Brother, stir and my mood further blackened. He was up, his hot, stinky breath breezing across my bare shoulder in an instant. That's one of the things I never liked about Brother, his agility and speed. I turned to face him, and it was then, in that instant, that I recognized where my evil mood had come from.

Brother and I, who'd spent our entire lives looking very much the opposite, awoke that morning of our 13th birthday, completely changed. We were mirrored images, our faces reflecting like rippling water upon each other. I was stunned, dumbfounded by the over-night metamorphism. He was too. We stared speechless at each other, moving in slow motion toward the middle of our room to touch each other's face and hair - even examine identical teeth in sour mouths. My fingers trembled against his skin and for just a second I saw fear in his eyes too.

"AUNT CHARLIE," I yelled, staring into Brother's dark brown eyes. "AUNT CHARLIE, I think you better get up here."

The panic in my voice brought Charlie racing up the stairs. The sweet smell of cinnamon and nutmeg followed his large hips into our bedroom where he promptly tripped over a pair of Brother's blue jeans left carelessly on the floor. I would have laughed if I wasn't so terrified by our surprising re-birth. Aunt Charlie's mouth fell open and he stared at each of us, his large hands turning us round like we mannequins in a department store display.

"Faces done finally caught up to your souls," Aunt Charlie said finally, smiling wide. He smashed our twin faces against the soft false breasts he adorned every morning. My heart pounded like a sledgehammer against the walls of my chest as I fought back the tears gathering in the corner of eyes. It had been a long time since I felt that kind of fear, firm and gripping, and I knew it wouldn't be letting me go anytime soon.

Warm June sunlight streamed through our bedroom window falling like a golden shadow upon my dark brown skin. To my natural eye the room appeared just the same, my half neat and clean, his side tossed and wrinkled with candy wrappers and book reports scattered about. My evil mood crawled all over me as I watched them walk down the stairs together talking about birthday cakes and gifts. Joy floated in their voices as I fought an overwhelming feeling of dread. Change was sure gonna come, I just knew it.

Author's Bio

Tina Smith-Brown is a writer, workshop leader and graphic artist. She is a graduate of Temple University's Journalism Program, the Art Institute Online, and currently working on her Graduate Degree in Creative Writing from University College, a division of Denver University. Tina is a recipient of a Pennsylvania Council of the Arts Fellowship and two Leeway Foundation Art and Change Awards. Fish and Grits is her first independently published novel and she is currently working on the sequel - *Brother*. She grew up in the Fairhill Housing Project, and currently lives in Northern Liberties.

Tina can be contacted through her Web Site creativetina.com, face book page- FishandGrits Novel, or her blog, run2fishandgrits.blogspot.com.